Even Yuppies Die

MARIAN BABSON

Even Yuppies Die

M
BABSON

ST. MARTIN'S PRESS ❦ NEW YORK

"A Thomas Dunne Book"

ISBN 0-312-13969-1

First published in Great Britain by
HarperCollins*Publishers*

First U.S. Edition: January 1996
10   9   8   7   6   5   4   3   2   1

Even Yuppies Die

CHAPTER 1

At the end of a long, hard day, there is nothing to quicken the footsteps and send the adrenalin coursing through the system like turning a corner and seeing three fire-engines and an ambulance standing outside your block of flats.

The girl on the pavement broke into a loping run, her face suddenly distorted with anxiety.

Inside our taxi, Jasper leaned forward and began hammering on the sliding glass panel separating us from the driver. 'Faster,' he shouted. 'Faster!'

'Unstable,' Evangeline murmured disapprovingly. 'The whole family was always unstable.' She had not noticed the fire-engines yet and I decided not to point them out. She was going to discover them soon enough.

'Faster, I said!' The taxi-driver was not responding quickly enough to Jasper's urgent command.

'Take it easy, guv.' In fact, the driver sounded distinctly unsympathetic. 'Can't plough through them engines, can I? There's laws about things like that.'

The running girl was moving faster than we were now. If Jasper didn't stop antagonizing the taxi-driver, we'd soon come to a complete halt.

'Fast— Oh, never mind!' Jasper began wrenching at the door-handle, but the little red light was still on, signalling that we were locked in. 'Let me out! That's *my* building! Let me out!'

The driver slammed on the brake and released the lock so abruptly that Jasper almost tumbled out into the street. He caught his balance and hit the ground running.

I leaped out behind him and followed. Behind me, I could hear Evangeline complaining:

'The luggage. You can't run off and leave me with all the . . .'

Jasper and the running girl reached the entrance to the building in a dead heat. I wasn't so far behind them.

As I threaded my way through the milling firemen, I felt that there was something familiar about the wide arched entrance, reached by two wide and shallow semi-circular marble steps.

A young man sat slumped in a corner of the top step, hunched over to hold a packet of frozen peas wrapped around one ankle. As we reached him, he lifted his head and his top lip curled back in a snarl.

'Nigel!' the girl said. 'What—?'

'Don't ask!' The snarl grew more pronounced. 'Don't even *think* of asking!' He struggled to his feet and limped into the building with as much dignity as he could muster, which wasn't much considering that he was bent almost double trying to keep the packet of frozen peas in place around his ankle.

One of the paramedics from the ambulance followed him unobtrusively but purposefully; he was carrying an elastic bandage obviously intended to replace the frozen peas.

'What's going on here?' Jasper whirled to address one of the firemen who seemed to be in charge.

'Nothing now.' The other firemen were beginning to roll up their hoses. 'It's all over. Don't worry. Not much damage.'

I made a mental bet that, as in the States, most of the damage would be water damage from all those hoses. And some smoke damage. The acrid reek hung heavy in the air and there was a faint grey haze just inside the front door.

'Am I to understand, my dear Jasper—' Evangeline was suddenly behind us, her voice dripping with venom—'that you are proposing to domicile us in a burning building?'

'It wasn't burning when I left it.' Jasper was immediately on the defensive.

Evangeline snorted dismissively and I saw her point. In the length of time that had elapsed since Jasper had met our train at King's Cross Station, taken us to an intimate little dinner—over which he had tried to explain the situation we had returned to—in an exclusive restaurant and organized another taxi to bring us, with all our luggage, to our new residence, half of London had had time to burn down.

'What happened here?' Jasper turned back to the fireman, who was easier to face than Evangeline.

'Chip pan fire.' The fireman glanced wryly at the elaborate building. 'Happens in the best of places.'

The taxi-driver had appeared, laden with our luggage. He grinned happily at the official verdict.

Behind us, one of the fire-engines silently pulled out from the kerb and rolled away. Other firemen were already boarding the second engine, their work accomplished.

The young woman switched her briefcase from one hand to the other, it seemed to be very full and very heavy; the brassbound corners would add to the weight, although they looked very chic. She glanced after the departing Nigel and then turned back to us. To Jasper, rather.

'Jasper—' she began, but he was still talking to the fireman and was unaware of her small voice.

'Jasper—' She tried again, a bit louder.

He still didn't hear her—or pretended not to—but I noticed that one shoulder twitched uneasily.

She sighed and, slumping into a waiting position, eased her left foot out of its expensive shoe. Immediately, the whole effect she had been presenting was ruined. She was wearing one of those short-black-skirt-and-long-black-jacket outfits that, as surely as Rosalind Russell's squared-off shoulder pads, signalled here was a Serious Career

Woman. All that was missing was the horn-rimmed glasses—the ones Cary Grant leaned over and gently removed before discovering, 'Why, Miss Jones, you're beautiful!' Something in the way she was blinking made me suspect that the glasses had been replaced by contact lenses. I suppose it's progress, but the hero leaning over and popping out the heroine's contact lenses just wouldn't have the same effect.

However, she was looking at Jasper as though he *was* Cary Grant. Jasper was looking through her as though she wasn't there at all.

'Jasper—' She caught him by the arm as he turned away from the fireman. He couldn't ignore that. 'Jasper, I *must* speak to you.'

'Not now, Mariah!' Jasper shook off her hand. 'I've got to get Trixie and Evangeline settled in the penthouse. They've had a long, tiring day travelling down from Whitby.'

'Oh yes.' She gave us a half-hearted smile, trying to act as though she hadn't been snubbed.

'Why don't you introduce us, Jasper?' If he could be rude, so could I. 'Isn't this one of our new neighbours?'

'Oh. Of course. Forgive me.' Jasper spoke to me and not the girl. 'Trixie, Evangeline, this is Mariah . . .' He hesitated. The look he gave her was every bit as hostile as the look Nigel-whoever-he-was had shot at her as he limped back to his smouldering chip pan. 'Mariah Lacey. Mariah, this is—'

'Oh, I know who you are,' Mariah said to us. 'Jasper has told us all about you.'

The statement did nothing to endear her to Jasper. Especially as Evangeline aimed a raised eyebrow at him and demanded, 'Such as what?'

'I only mentioned that you'd be staying here, that's all.' Jasper's glare defied Mariah to contradict him.

'Oh yes. Yes, that's right.' Mariah smiled nervously. 'Jasper, if we could just decide a time for a meeting—?'

I yawned. I couldn't help it. We'd started out early that morning, taking a tiny little train that seemed to meander through half the back yards from Whitby to Middlesbrough, where we changed to the big Intercity Express to London. It had been an endless five hours, not improved by the lack of a dining car. Fortunately, dear Meta had insisted on packing a delicious lunch box for us, but the restiveness of passengers who had been foolish enough to depend on the Buffet Car had added to the vague discomfort of the journey.

'You're tired,' Jasper noticed, quite as though he had not had anything to do with it. Kind though it was of him to meet our train at King's Cross and take us to dinner, we could have done without it. We had been thinking longingly of a hot bath and an early night. Well, perhaps a bowl of hot soup or something first.

'Exhausted,' I agreed. There is nothing more exhausting than sharing a meal with a man who has an axe to grind— and Jasper had ground it relentlessly over dinner. He appeared to imagine that we were in constant contact with his grandparents and would report to them on his movements. Hence, he spent a lot of time trying to justify his current position—in which we had no interest, except for the fact that we would no longer be living in St John's Wood.

He had jabbered frantically about investments that had gone wrong, forcing him to borrow more money on the St John's Wood property, then things had gone worse . . . repossession . . . but all was not lost. There was this absolutely super warehouse in Docklands he was remodelling to the highest luxury standard and, fortunately, there was a spare apartment we could move into.

We weren't absolutely delighted but, so long as we had

a place to lay our weary heads tonight, we weren't going
to worry about anything until morning. Whatever had happened was Jasper's problem and he could sort it out with
Beau and Juanita for himself.

'What are we waiting for?' Evangeline demanded. 'Are
we to spend the night stretched out on the floor of this
marble mausoleum?'

'No, no, of course not.' Jasper was galvanized into action.
'I told you, you're in the penthouse.' He led the way to a
pair of elevators on the far side of the lobby, past a sweeping
flight of marble stairs. 'You have your own private lift—
and it's working.'

'Why shouldn't it be?' Evangeline was immediately suspicious. 'Did the fire department short-circuit the wiring?'

She had a point. The lobby was unnaturally dim. Either
something had gone wrong with the system and the emergency lighting had kicked in, or the lowest possible wattage
bulbs were in the sockets.

'Everything's fine.' Jasper was looking increasingly
harassed, perhaps because Mariah was right on our heels.
He stabbed at a call button and a door slid open instantly.
We stepped into the sleek mirrored interior, trying not to
notice how bedraggled we looked.

'Jasper, please—' Mariah looked at him imploringly.

'Tomorrow.' He stabbed at another button, not looking
at her. 'Tomorrow without fail.'

'You said that yester—' The door closed in her face. We
shot upwards.

Although a swift ride, it was a silent one. Jasper stared
at the door like a man trapped in an elevator with embar-
rassing strangers and just waiting for the release of the door
opening again at his floor.

Once the door opened, however, he was himself again,
leading us out into a small foyer with brocade-panelled
walls and a door opening off it in each corner.

'There are four penthouse suites, actually,' Jasper said, opening one of the doors. 'Two large and two small. This is the biggest, with the best view. The buyer will have the option of buying one of the smaller ones for a guest annexe, or perhaps for the servants. I'm occupying one of them myself temporarily.'

We followed him into an inner foyer which opened out into an enormous room. A wall of windows gave it the feeling of being suspended in space, with the glittering panorama of the lights of London spreading out in the distance below.

'Just a minute,' Jasper said. I heard switches clicking. 'Ah, that's better.'

Better than what? A dim glow suffused the wall and a small area around it. There was more light from the almost-full moon outside.

'I didn't know they still made twenty-watt bulbs,' Evangeline said.

'They're on a dimmer.' Jasper fiddled with the switch again. 'That's the Twilight Effect, so that you can appreciate the view.' The dim radiance grew brighter; they made forty-watt bulbs, too.

'You couldn't read a newspaper by that light,' Evangeline jeered. 'Not even the headlines.'

'At the end of a long working day at the computer—' Jasper spoke with painful dignity—'people don't want to read. They want to be soothed, to look out over the City and dream.'

So where were these people? And where were their dreams? It sounded as though Jasper had fallen victim to his own publicity handouts—a not-unknown fate in Hollywood. The hard-working dreamers who were prepared to house their servants in an adjoining penthouse suite had manifestly failed to materialize. Otherwise, Evangeline and I would not now be housed in such empty, echoing splendour. A magnificent view was all very well, but one did cherish hopes that there would be a couple of beds hidden away somewhere.

As my eyes grew accustomed to the faint light, I was cheered to discern familiar pieces of furniture dotted around the great room like tiny islands marooned in space. The place may have cried out for Scandinavian *moderne*, but the old red plush Victorian sofa from St John's Wood looked mighty good to me right now. I made a beeline for it and sank on to it. Evangeline found one of the armchairs and kicked off her shoes.

'Um, yes,' Jasper said. 'Actually, I was going to show you where everything is.'

'Just point out the bedrooms, dear boy,' Evangeline said. 'We'll find everything else for ourselves. In the morning.'

'Yes, well, I'll put your cases in your rooms.' Jasper admitted defeat.

Evangeline and I watched as he carried our suitcases into adjoining rooms. He still seemed vaguely dissatisfied. Maybe we should have shown more enthusiasm about the building, or the penthouse, or something—but it had been a long day. Besides, there was still a faint smell of smoke in the air—and a reception by fire-engines does tend to dampen one's enthusiasm for new surroundings. Abruptly, I wished we were back in the house in St John's Wood.

'Umm, well . . .' Jasper emerged empty-handed from the second bedroom and stood staring at us uneasily.

'The word you're groping for, dear boy, is "good night"', Evangeline told him.

'Yes, well . . . if you need anything, I'm right across the hall.'

'I can't tell you how much that reassures us.' She let her voice frost over as he continued to hover by the door. 'Good night.'

'Yes. I—I was just wondering . . . Are you still friends with that policeman?'

'Which one?' I asked.

'Why?' Evangeline went straight to the point.

'Uuuuh . . . Good night.' Jasper had finally mastered his line. Also the fact that it was an exit line. 'Good night!' He rushed for the door and we heard it slam behind him.

Evangeline and I looked at each other blankly. Another slam, following like an echo upon the first, told us that he was safe in his own penthouse.

'Now what—?'

I forced myself to my feet and headed in the direction of the room where Jasper had dumped my suitcases. Suddenly, I felt at one with our new neighbour on the front step. Except for the frozen peas.

'Don't even *think* of asking,' I said.

CHAPTER 2

I opened my eyes to the reflection of rippling water on the ceiling. For a traitorous moment, I thought I was back in my old home in Beverly Hills with the swimming pool just under the bedroom windows, so that the more adventurous guests could dive straight in before breakfast. The room was flooded with a light so bright I found it hard to recognize it—it had been a long time since I had seen the sun.

Then I heard a crash and an explosive oath in the distance and I woke up a bit more and remembered where I was. I closed my eyes and turned over.

But I couldn't close my ears. After a few more crashes my nerves couldn't stand it, so I threw back the covers, struggled into my dressing-gown and followed the sound of breaking crockery.

'This kitchen is so high-tech you need a Ph.D in physics to boil an egg,' Evangeline complained in greeting. 'If you could find an egg.'

'Aren't there any curtains in this place?' I had a complaint of my own as I narrowed my eyes against the dazzle of sunlight on highly-polished metal all over the room. Even the table and chairs were constructed of bright tubes in a sort of Charles Rennie Mackintosh meets Cape Canaveral fantasy. I hoped they were more comfortable to sit on than they looked.

'Curtains are expensive.' Evangeline abstractedly looked at a cup handle she was still inexplicably holding between her fingers—the rest of the cup was in large shards at her feet—then pitched it into a corner on top of an obviously growing pile of broken dishes. She was neat, in her fashion.

'I suppose Jasper thinks we're so high up we don't need curtains here. It's not as though anyone else could look in.'

'Jasper . . .' Evangeline said broodingly. 'I intend to have a word with that young man.'

'I hope you have better luck than that girl last night. He's pretty fast on his feet.'

'With good reason, I suspect.' She started forward and seemed surprised when her foot crunched down on the remains of the cup. She looked at the shards thoughtfully for a moment, then, with the unerring accuracy that had made her name a byword for terror at countless croquet tournaments in the days when they had been all the rage, executed a quick series of chip-shots with her toe to send the pieces skittering into the pile in the corner. She then continued on her way, ignoring the residue of flakes and powder still scattered on the floor.

'Where's the broom?' I sighed. If I didn't clean that up, some would get ground into the flooring and the rest would get tracked all over the apartment.

'If this establishment doesn't run to curtains, what on

earth makes you imagine there'd be a broom?' Evangeline gazed around with dissatisfaction. 'Personally, I'd be happy if we could just identify the fridge. Assuming that there *is* one.'

'There must be!' I looked more closely at the State-of-the-Art kitchen. All the equipment seemed to be built into the walls. Could they do that with a fridge?

There were enough dials and control panels to send a spaceship into orbit. I wondered if even Martha would be able to feel competent in a kitchen like this. I could just about make a guess at which bit might possibly be the microwave oven—but I wouldn't like to put it to the test without an engineer standing by.

All those shining steel poles framed vast expanses of smoked glass—the I-can-see-you-but-you-can't-look-at-me, you-peasant type, always seen in the limousines of rock stars and minor diplomats. Lurking somewhere behind the glass there must be a proper oven, and perhaps even a fridge. But the smoked glass was not about to yield up its secrets to a casual observer. This whole kitchen ought to come with operating instructions.

Meanwhile, there should be a broom or even a vacuum cleaner somewhere. Maybe the broom closet also concealed the refrigerator and other homely household appliances. There was a door in the corner: wooden, with a real doorknob, looking oddly out of place in these futuristic surroundings. Perhaps it was part of the original warehouse. That was promising; it might lead into a good old-fashioned closet.

I opened the door, stepped forward—and screamed.

'Careful!' Evangeline leaped across the room and grabbed my arm.

'EEEeeek!' I stared into empty space. 'There's no floor there!' Instead, there was a sheer drop of about three storeys—straight down.

'I was about to mention that.' Evangeline tugged me back into the kitchen and slammed the door against the abyss.

'But — But — That's dangerous!' I was miserably aware of sounding like an idiot. 'There ought to be a key. That door should be kept locked!'

'I agree,' Evangeline said grimly. She swung one of the chairs over to block the door. 'It's one of the points I intend to take up with Jasper.'

'Just one?' What else was wrong around here?

'Get dressed, Trixie. We're going *out* to breakfast.'

But that was easier said than done.

'Water, water, everywhere . . .' Evangeline murmured as we stood outside the front entrance and looked around.

'"A sleepy lagoon . . ."' I hummed, topping her. We hadn't had a chance to see anything at all last night. Not only had it been too dark, but the fire-engines had been in the way.

Now we found ourselves looking down on a narrow street with a wide stretch of river beyond it; there was a narrow walkway along the river side. The converted warehouse fronted on the Thames and on one side of the building was a deep inlet which had presumably served as an additional dock in the days when the warehouse was in service. There was another narrow walkway curving between the side of the warehouse and the retaining wall of the dock.

The only sound was the quiet lap of water against the embankment. We were the only people in sight. We might have been miles out in the country. Or on another planet. Suddenly, all that quiet began to get on my nerves.

'Maybe if we go a little farther along.' There was no restaurant in sight—nor any shops, come to think of it. 'We might find something . . .' My voice trailed off; I was no longer so sure.

The next building to ours was a derelict warehouse with a large sign tilting precariously away from one of the upper levels. 'UNDER OFFER' it proclaimed optimistically. Judging from the tilt of the sign and the amount of sea-gull droppings obscuring the print, the offer had never materialized in any final form.

'And perhaps we should walk on the other side of the street.' Evangeline eyed the sign mistrustfully. 'There appears to be a sidewalk over there, such as it is.'

'Good idea.' A slight breeze had sprung up and the sign began swaying. The river rippled and sparkled. It was really more of a wind than a breeze and really quite cold. In a moment of *déjà vu* for the recent past, I wished we were still wearing our merino wool costumes.

'Brr!' Evangeline, too, felt the chill. 'Let's keep moving. If we head upriver, we'll at least be going in the right direction. The West End is up there somewhere.'

'Not within walking distance, I'm afraid.' We crossed over to the river sidewalk and stood at the railing for a moment. 'That taxi last night seemed to have travelled an awfully long way.'

'*That* looks like a restaurant!' Evangeline had looked over the railing down at the river below us where a houseboat was moored. There was a sign on top proclaiming it to be *The Gliding Gourmet*.

'It looks promising,' I agreed, 'but it doesn't look open. It probably just serves dinners.' I looked at the sign again. Why the *Gliding?* 'Maybe with river trips included.'

'They might do lunches as well.' Evangeline moved forward, impelled by hope. 'It's nearly lunch-time.'

'I don't know.' I followed along doubtfully. 'There don't seem to be any businesses along here.'

'People work from home these days.' Evangeline dismissed my doubts. 'All those fax machines and computer terminals . . .'

Maybe, but it still didn't add up to a lunch-time rush. We found the steps leading down to the dock but, the closer we got, the more shut-down *The Gliding Gourmet* looked. I was beginning to suspect that it was an ex-restaurant, maybe even as derelict as the old warehouse we had just passed.

'Well . . .' Evangeline slowed her pace. We could see the gilt peeling from the sign now. Curtains hung limp and defeated at the window. A large padlock secured the door.

'Well, that takes care of that bright idea.' Evangeline glared at me as though I had been the one to raise her hopes. 'Now what do we do?'

'I guess we keep right on walking.' The prospect was not pleasing. I realized I had allowed my own hopes to rise too far.

Gloomily, we went back up the steps and trudged along. There was a bend in the river just ahead. I tried not to visualize a marina of shops, snack bars and restaurants lurking beyond it.

I was right. Nothing but more converted warehouses and water, water, everywhere, as Evangeline had so aptly remarked. There were banners attached to most of the warehouses, advising that one-two-and-three-bedroom flats were still available at premium rates. The banners flapped dispiritedly in the breeze, grey-tinged and weather-beaten.

At least the wind was behind us, chill and cutting though it was. What else could one expect beside the river in the dying days of January?

But the wind wasn't all that was behind us, I realized suddenly, with an additional chill down my spine.

Clop-clump, clop-clump . . . the uneven footfalls were gaining on us. I braced myself and turned around. The limping jogger faltered and slowed, frowning as though trying to place us.

'Hello, Nigel,' I said. 'How's your ankle this morning?'

'Better, thanks.' His face cleared. 'Ah! Yes! You're Jasper's friends. You've taken the penthouse.'

'We've had it thrust upon us,' Evangeline muttered, but Nigel wasn't listening.

Neither was I. For a moment, I was afraid that hunger was inducing auditory hallucinations. I heard a telephone ringing. Right there on the walkway.

'Excuse me—' Nigel slipped a backpack off his shoulders and, to my relief, brought out a portable telephone. He pushed a button and barked, 'Colroy Consultancy, Colroy here.' He was silent, his frown growing as he listened to the voice at the other end.

'Not now, Mariah. I'm busy!' He snapped the connection off, returned the phone to his knapsack and breathed heavily for a moment before regaining his composure and smiling at us with somewhat frayed urbanity.

'We hadn't a chance to meet properly last night.' He rummaged in his backpack and brought out a card. 'Nigel Colroy, Investment Counsellor.' He looked at us hopefully.

'How do you do.' Evangeline took the card and slid it into her handbag to join all the others that accumulated there until the combined weight prompted her to have a clear-out. Then she just upended the bag over the nearest wastebasket.

'Any time I can be of service to you . . .' Not guessing the eventual fate of his business card, he seemed to think he was in with a chance.

'Is there some place to eat around here?' My blood sugar level was so low it was lying in folds around my ankles. I was getting so desperate I'd have cheerfully gnawed a few frozen peas, but Nigel wasn't using his emergency ice-pack today.

'Ah! Yes! I mean, no! Not really. Not in the immediate vicinity. Not now.' He followed Evangeline's glance towards *The Gliding Gourmet*. 'That's only open at weekends

now . . . and then only for dinner. And not every weekend
at that.' He frowned. 'It's too bad. It did a raging business
at first, but then money got tight.'

'Yes, people can cook their own meals much more econ-
omically.' Restaurant prices in this country had already
horrified me.

'If they don't set the place on fire cooking it!' Evangeline
had not forgotten the chip-pan fire—nor forgiven it.

'Ah! Yes! Sorry about that. I don't usually do my own
cooking, but Sandra, my . . . partner . . . left—just for a
few days, I'm sure. Unexpectedly—' He seemed to realize
that he was gabbling—and perhaps giving away too much.

'She'll be back.' He sounded as though he was trying
to convince himself more than us. 'Soon, I hope. Then
everything will be back to normal and there won't be any
more culinary mishaps. I hope.'

'I'm sure everyone hopes that,' Evangeline said grimly.
It sounded as though Nigel had been deserted and had
better sign up for a cooking course, if only for the sake of
the other residents.

'Fortunately, one does carry insurance against these accidents.' He seemed to find a silver lining. 'Although actually,
there wasn't much damage.' He frowned. 'The fire department got here very quickly. Of course—' he brightened—
'I haven't finished assessing the water damage yet.'

'Water . . .' Evangeline brooded out over the shimmering surface, now no longer so far below us. 'Speaking
of which, this river seems to be getting rather high.'

'The tide is coming in. The Thames is a tidal river.' Nigel
seemed pleased at the change of subject. 'It rises and falls
with the tide, twice a day. The water can almost reach the
top of the parapet at times.'

'Gosh!' I looked at the high water mark just below us.
It seemed very close, too close for comfort. 'What if there's
a flood tide?'

'Oh, you don't have to worry about floods. Not any more. We have the Thames Barrier now. Eighth Wonder of the World, it's claimed. Any danger of flooding and they close the gates. No more floods for London. That's why water-front property is such a good investment now.' It sounded like another thing he was trying to convince himself about. 'That is, all other things being equal.'

'What about food? Breakfast?' Evangeline brought us back to the main concern.

'Ah! Yes! Actually, there are a couple of places—but they're on the other side of the river.'

'And is there a ferry to take us across?'

'Ah! No!'

'Mmm . . .' Evangeline had suspected as much. 'Then where is the nearest place on this side of the river?'

'Ah! Well, there's a working-men's caff, but I wouldn't really recommend it—and it's not all that near, at that. Tell you what—' His face cleared and he groped for his cellphone again. 'Why don't I ring for a taxi to come and collect you? Then you can go straight to the West End and have your choice of any number of restaurants.'

'It seems,' Evangeline said, as Nigel made the arrangements, 'there's something to be said for those contraptions, after all.'

CHAPTER 3

Breakfast was luncheon by the time we got it, but the Savoy did a lot towards restoring our equilibrium.

'Maybe—' It was worth a try. 'Maybe we could move in here for a couple of weeks while we house-hunt.'

'I think not!' The waiter had just discreetly set down the bill in front of Evangeline and she looked at it and paled, even though the prices had been clearly set out on the menu. 'Jasper collected another quarter's rent in advance from us before we went up to Whitby and we are going to get our money's worth.' Evangeline's lips tightened grimly. 'We may not be in the premises we paid for, but paid for they are and we shall remain until the end of the quarter— or until Jasper gives us a refund.'

'I don't think that's very likely.' In fact, I suspected that Jasper had blown all his available cash on the taxis last night. He had charged dinner at the restaurant, tossing his credit card on to the table with the same rakehell defiant flourish his grandfather had used in *King of the Riverboat Gamblers* when he bet his dying wife's emerald earrings on one last desperate turn of the cards.

'It wouldn't surprise me—' Evangeline seemed to pick up on my thoughts—'to learn that that young man is even deeper in debt than we think. And Beau is too far away to bail him out.'

'In the unlikely event that he felt so inclined.' Beau was notoriously tight with a dollar, pound, franc, escudo, or whatever currency he was presently wrestling with. He would not be pleased to return and discover the extent of his grandson's financial downfall.

'If you want to stay there for the time being, it's OK with me, but I think we ought to at least start looking around for another place. It may take a while.'

'Nonsense, Trixie! We should have no trouble finding something suitable—when we're ready. We can't waste time on that now. The first priority is to get back on stage. It's obvious that we can't depend on Hugh to help us. We'll have to sort it out for ourselves.'

'When Hugh and Martha get back from their honeymoon—' I began.

Evangeline gave me the kind of look that said she wasn't going to dignify that remark by replying to it, dropped her money beside mine and stood up.

I sighed silently and followed her from the dining-room, smiling absently to the bowing waiters. She really had a down on poor Hugh and it was getting worse. I decided to be elsewhere for their first meeting after his return.

It was still cold outside, but considerably warmer than it had been in Docklands with the wind blowing straight off the river.

'We'll walk,' Evangeline said as the doorman offered her a cab. 'This is part of my old stamping grounds; I'd like to see what changes there have been.'

We walked through the forecourt and out into the Strand. She stopped, looking up and down the street.

'Yes, yes. Simpson's is still here. And the Adelphi and the Vaudeville. The Civil Service Store has gone, but the dear old Strand Palace Hotel is still here.' She sighed nostalgically.

'Let's walk up towards Drury Lane and the Aldwych. There are more theatres there and—' a gleam came into her eye—'it's matinee day. We should be able to get in somewhere and see how full the houses are.'

'Sounds good to me.' After our exile in the Northern wastes, I was all for anything that would keep us in the heart of a city again.

We crossed the Strand and turned towards Drury Lane, then halted on the corner of a one-way street while the wind off the river found us again. I turned away and saw the tall, once-white columns supporting the marquee of a deserted theatre. Tattered posters could not disguise its seedy grandeur. I read the name and gasped.

'Yes, the Lyceum,' Evangeline said. 'Where Sir Henry Irving trod the boards at the height of his career—and Bram Stoker worked back of the house as his Manager.'

'Henry Irving!' I looked at the flaking paint on the façade. '*And* Bram Stoker was working there when he wrote *Dracula?*'

'Before, during and after—that's where it all started.
Small world, Trixie, with two legends in the same place at
the same time.'

This is one of the things about England. There you are,
strolling along, minding your own business—and suddenly,
History reaches out and taps you on the shoulder.

'Historic ground, Trixie. A place of theatrical legend—
and look at the way they've let it go to seed!'

'Disgraceful!' I could hardly believe it, but my eyes told
me it was true. 'One of the most beautiful and historic
theatres in London, falling to ruin.'

'There hasn't been a theatrical performance in it since
God-knows-when. Sheer waste! And all the Government,
Council and Preservationists do is talk. I'd like to horse-
whip everyone concerned!'

Brrr!' It wasn't the emotion that made me shudder, the
wind was suddenly sharper.

'Quick, we've got the light now.' We dashed across Well-
ington Street and were immediately confronted by another
theatre, a whole cluster of theatres.

'The Duchess, the Theatre Royal, the Strand and the
Aldwych!' Evangeline took a deep breath, as though she
could smell the greasepaint in the air. 'Oh, the memories!'
She looked fondly at the Strand Theatre on the corner.
'Dear Ivor Novello had his own flat right at the top. It was
ideal. After the performance, all he had to do was go
upstairs and he was home.'

We both brooded silently for a moment on this blissful
ideal.

'Home . . . with London at his feet. And oh! the parties
he gave there!'

'Lucky old you,' I sighed. 'I never got to Europe until
the war—and our USO tour only stopped in London long
enough for a briefing before we went on to the Continent.'

'They were great days, Trixie.' Evangeline sighed in her

turn, then her attention was caught by a sign across the road. 'Do you see what I see?'

'MATINEE TODAY' the sign proclaimed. 'Over 1000 performances . . . London's longest-running farce . . .'

'Looks good to me.' We started forward eagerly. There were already people milling about in the theatre lobby and on the pavement. Taxis had begun drawing up and discharging groups of women, who then clustered together amiably squabbling over their share of the fare.

The scene was so familiar it felt like coming home. I quickened my footsteps, wanting to be part of it again.

So did Evangeline. We dashed across the street in a dead heat while a taxi indignantly sounded its horn as it had to brake to avoid hitting us. We gained the kerb outside the theatre, laughing.

There was only a short queue at the box office and we joined it. A buzz of excitement humming through the lobby told us we had been recognized. It was hardly a moment before the House Manager materialized beside us.

'Miss Sinclair, Miss Dolan, we're honoured. You'll have our House Seats, of course.' He waved away any attempt to pay him. 'And perhaps you'd like to join me in the interval for a drink . . .'

The letdown set in in the taxi going back to Docklands. As we drove out of the centre of the city and through the endless commercial districts, the temperature dropped about ten degrees and it began to seem as though we were heading for Siberia.

By the time the taxi stopped in front of our building, it was a toss-up as to which of us was in a worse mood.

'This it?' The taxi-driver wasn't any happier himself. He gazed at the YUPPIE SCUM OUT! scrawl on the building as though he agreed with it. I hadn't noticed it before and it added to the vague disquiet I already felt.

'Good job it's still early,' the driver grumbled. 'You'd have a time getting a taxi out here late at night. Too far out—and the tips are no good any more, what with the recession and all.'

'See to it, Trixie!' Evangeline hurled over her shoulder at me as she got out and hurried up the steps and into the shelter of the lobby.

'Never mind, love.' The taxi-driver consoled me while I fumbled for change. 'It's better than the Embankment.'

He had driven off before it occurred to me that, thanks to Evangeline's tone of voice, he had mistaken me for an indigent relative living off Evangeline's bounty—and paying for it by doing companion/maid service. I was so annoyed that I stumbled on the lower of the entrance steps.

'I say, watch it!' My arm was caught and held, steadying me. I looked up into the pleasant face of a young man in a pin-striped suit and bowler hat, carrying what seemed to be the obligatory brass-bound attaché case in his other hand.

'Thank you,' I said. 'I'm all right now.'

'Good, good.' He moved quickly to swing the door open for me with exaggerated courtesy. I began to suspect that he had witnessed the scene Evangeline had just played and had jumped to the same conclusion as the taxi-driver. 'Staying here, are you?'

'We're in the penthouse,' I said coldly. Evangeline was already over at the elevators, pushing buttons impatiently.

'Neighbours, then.' Still holding my arm protectively, he walked over with me. 'I'm a couple of floors below. They hadn't finished the penthouse suites when we bought. Just as well.' He gave a small unamused laugh. 'We couldn't afford them anyway.'

They still hadn't finished, but I didn't feel like telling him that.

'You took your time,' Evangeline greeted me ungraciously, still sounding like an arrogant employer of ungrateful insubordinates. She looked pointedly at the hand on my arm. 'Aren't you going to introduce us?'

'I would if I could,' I said, equally pointedly.

'Oh, forgive me. I'm Hamish Atherton. I live in sixty-three-B.'

'*And* you're a friend of Jasper's, no doubt,' Evangeline said in tones that damned him.

'Yes, as a matter of fact. We went to school together.'

Evangeline sniffed and turned away. Any friend of Jasper's, her attitude conveyed clearly, was an idiot.

'Sixty-three-B,' he repeated, gazing at me intently. '"The Chummery" we call it, after the shared bachelor quarters in the days of the old British Raj. Four of us share—and it's always Open House. My friends are always welcome to drop in and escape—' his glance flicked lightly at Evangeline—'their cares. Any time at all.'

'That's very kind of you.' The offer had to be acknowledged and—who knows?—I might be glad of a chance to escape from Evangeline occasionally, even if not for the reason he thought.

Our private elevator to the penthouse reached us first and its doors glided open. At the same moment, the front door opened across the lobby and a young woman entered.

'Quick!' Suddenly, Hamish's gallantry disappeared as he leaped into the lift ahead of us. 'Get in!' he whispered urgently. 'Get in!'

We had barely cleared the threshold when he began stabbing frantically at the CLOSE DOOR button.

'Hamish . . .' A voice came faintly to us. 'Hamish, is that you?' Hurrying footsteps clicked across the lobby. 'Wait a minute . . .'

The door shut silently and the lift began to move

upwards. Hamish sagged against the wall momentarily, weak with relief.

'Wasn't that Mariah?' I asked.

'Who? What?' His face assumed an expression of improbable innocence. 'Who?'

Evangeline and I exchanged glances.

'You're in the wrong lift,' Evangeline pointed out. 'This one is an express to the penthouse.'

'Is it?' His eyes widened, emphasizing his innocence, and he smiled ruefully. 'Never mind, I'll just walk down a couple of flights. It doesn't matter.'

But it would have mattered if he'd met Mariah. What on earth was wrong with that girl? So far, practically any man who came near her had all but held up a cross and waved garlic in her face. If she had been with us in Whitby, it might have been type-casting. And yet, she seemed like a perfectly normal friendly young woman. Obviously she had hidden depths, only visible to the male of the species.

'What floor is Mariah on?' Evangeline's curiosity was roused, as well.

'Oh, er, the fourth, I believe.' So he was safe from meeting her on the stairs.

'She owns her flat all by herself.' He sounded wistful. 'Most of us took joint mortgages with friends, so that we could afford a bigger and better apartment. It was an investment. How were we to know—?' He stopped and brightened. 'Anyway, her place is absolutely tiny compared to ours.'

For someone who only 'believed' her flat was on the fourth floor, he seemed to know a lot about it. Was Mariah the other party in a failed romance? With every man in the building?

The lift stopped and the door opened on our little foyer. Hamish stepped back to allow us to go out first. When it was his turn, he still hesitated.

'It's all right,' Evangeline said. 'The coast is clear.'

He strolled out pretending he didn't know what she was talking about, but his gaze flicked uneasily around the foyer. Then he crossed to one of the brocade panels and pushed it, revealing a flight of stairs.

'So there's a fire exit out here!' Evangeline exclaimed. 'Jasper might have told us!'

He certainly might, considering that the only other exit involved a three-storey drop from the kitchen door.

'Shouldn't there be a sign on it?' Evangeline asked.

'Oh, I think not.' He seemed vaguely affronted. 'This isn't a hotel, you know. Nor even a public building. You wouldn't have strangers wandering around up here and the people who live here don't need a sign. They know the concealed door leads to the stairs.'

'We do *now*.' I looked into the small hallway thus revealed and was interested to see that two other doors opened into it—one of which must, from its placement, lead out from our drawing-room. A closer investigation of our panelling was going to be high on my agenda. But it made sense. If the foyer were to be filled with smoke, a direct exit from the flat was obviously a good idea.

Thinking of smoke, I wondered if Nigel's girlfriend really was going to return to him and if he would continue to try to do his own cooking. And how about the other occupants? I wouldn't trust Hamish very far with a chip pan, either.

Hamish paused before closing the panel and gave me an earnest look. 'Remember,' he said meaningly. 'You'll always be welcome in sixty-three-B.'

'Well!' Evangeline said as the panel clicked shut. 'You've made a conquest!' She needn't have sounded so surprised about it.

I smiled enigmatically. I wouldn't give her the satisfaction of telling her the truth about what Hamish thought.

CHAPTER 4

The refurbishment of the old warehouse couldn't have been all that good. Otherwise, we wouldn't have been able to hear someone else's doorbell ringing so clearly that, for a moment, I thought it was our own.

'What's that infernal racket?' Evangeline complained.

'How do I know?' But I was already on my way to find out. I flicked the switch activating one of the pair of tiny TV security screens perched over the door. Immediately the foyer outside sprang into view (the other screen covered the front entrance downstairs) and I saw a familiar back. She was ringing Jasper's doorbell determinedly.

'Mariah—' I opened our own door and spoke to her.

'Where?' The girl whirled around and I saw that she was not Mariah. She wore the same sort of long tailored jacket and short skirt, but she was just another City clone in the standard uniform. She stared around wildly, looking frightened and at bay.

'Where's Mariah?' she demanded. 'Is she in there with you?'

'No, there's only Evangeline here with me.' I tried to be soothing, but a muffled snort from behind told me that Evangeline didn't appreciate that 'only'.

'I don't think Jasper's home.' I concentrated on reassuring the young woman, who did seem calmer now that she knew Mariah wasn't in the immediate offing. 'Would you like to leave a message with us?'

'No! Yes. No . . . I mean, would you tell him I need to speak to him? My . . . my heating has gone off.'

'All right.' It was not unknown for such a thing to happen, even in the best-run place—which this certainly wasn't—so why didn't I believe her? 'Er, I can't really tell him unless you give me your name.'

'Oh, sorry. I'm Roz Ross. I know who you are, of course. Jasper has been talking about you for weeks.'

'Has he?' Evangeline crowded into the doorway behind me. 'Dear Jasper, perhaps he missed his calling. He should have been a Press Agent.'

'Oh, you don't mind, do you?' Roz asked uncertainly. 'We're all so pleased and excited to have you here. And it's going to be such good publicity for selling—' She broke off, but not soon enough.

'You mean—' Evangeline pounced like a cat. 'You mean we're being used as shills to bring buyers into this empty building?'

'It's not empty. Not completely.'

'It's not finished, either.' Evangeline had her there.

'It will be. Just as soon as the cash flow improves—' She stopped and shook her head groggily, as though wondering how she had suddenly got into what was almost an argument with someone who was really a stranger. Evangeline often had that effect on people.

'Why don't you come in and sit down?' I invited. 'You can wait with us until Jasper comes home.' The girl was obviously a potential goldmine of information—if handled in the right way.

'No, no, thank you.' As I had feared, Evangeline had frightened her off. 'I must be going.'

'But you can't go back and sit in that cold apartment,' I cooed. 'It's nice and warm in our place.'

'I won't go back to the apartment,' she said. 'The supermarket is open until nine tonight and I ought to do some shopping anyway. By the time I've been round the supermarket, Jasper will probably be back.'

'Supermarket? Shopping?' I could feel my face light up. 'Do they have such things around here? We've been looking, but we haven't seen any shops at all. And we have no supplies—' I let my chin quiver and my voice quaver. 'Not even a loaf of bread or a carton of milk. We had to go out for breakfast this morning, but there aren't any restaurants around here, either. Where *is* this supermarket?'

'Actually, you need a car to get to it—' I could see her trying to harden her heart, but she was basically a nice well-brought-up girl and I'd dropped the hint hard enough to break her toe.

'If you'd like to come along,' she offered half-heartedly, 'I could show you where everything is and we could do our shopping together.'

'Wonderful! I'll just get my coat and purse and be right with you. Are you coming, Evangeline?'

'No, thank you.' Evangeline pretended not to hear the faint sigh of relief that escaped from the girl. 'I'll stay here and wait for Jasper. I'll give him your message,' she added sweetly to Roz.

After that, Roz and I got along just fine, although she was still on her guard. All the glittering nuggets of information remained potential, even though I dug to the best of my ability. She was willing to talk about anything except the warehouse and its inhabitants. I learned far more than I ever wanted to know about Docklands and its development. I was guided to the best buys in the supermarket, treated to coffee and cake in its snack bar, and regaled with anecdotes of her school and family life before she moved to London. I got the feeling that life had been happier in those days.

The friendliness slipped a little when we got back to the warehouse. Roz helped me carry my shopping-bags into the express lift and then—too quickly—accepted my assurance that I would be all right from there. She was still gunshy of Evangeline.

'Well—?' Evangeline demanded, opening the door to my ring. 'What did you find out?'

'I found out that it's going to take a taxi expedition every time we want to do any shopping.' I dropped the first two carrier bags inside the door. 'Come and help me unload the lift. I think maybe I overbought a bit. The excitement of all those shelves of groceries went to my head.'

'You have enough here to feed an army,' Evangeline grumbled as we ferried the loaded bags from the lift to the kitchen.

'I figured, who knows when I'll get to a supermarket again?' I began unpacking: 'And, in case you hadn't noticed, the cupboard—wherever it is—is absolutely bare.'

'Oh, well . . .' With unerring instinct, Evangeline had homed in on the carrier bag containing the brandy, Brie, assortment of pâtés, smoked salmon and Bath Olivers. She was becoming more mollified by the moment. 'I suppose we *do* need the essentials.'

'That's right.' I unpacked the two wine boxes and stored the white in the fridge, trying not to think about the last time we had done this. Then I stood holding the box of claret, wondering where would be the best place to store it. We wanted it at room temperature, but didn't want to open it immediately. At least, I didn't—and I noticed that Evangeline was already pouring herself a drink from the brandy bottle, so she wouldn't be interested, either.

I decided to put it down by the back door—the dangerous one—and froze.

Loud angry voices sounded as though they were having a fight just outside the door. But they couldn't be. There was nothing outside that door but empty space.

'Evangeline.' I found myself whispering. 'Come over here.'

'What is it?' Always ready for intrigue and responding to my cue, she tiptoed across the floor to stand beside me.

'Listen!'

The voices rose and fell, the fury evident, the words blurred.

'Open the door,' Evangeline said. 'We can hear better.'

'Do you think we should?' Belatedly, my conscience assailed me.

Evangeline moved the guarding chair aside, reached across me and turned the knob, silently pulling the door open a good six inches. We bent forward eagerly, the words were clearer now. Not all of them, but some of them . . .

'. . . won't let . . . do this . . .'

'. . . can't stop me . . .'

'. . . law . . .'

'. . . *my* side . . .'

It was infuriating. To be able to hear so much—and yet so little. And not to be able to identify the voices. Of course, we hadn't met most of the occupants of the building yet. But . . . was there something vaguely familiar about one of the men's voices? Or was it just that all upper class English male voices sounded vaguely alike?

Evangeline opened the door wider and leaned out.

'Be careful!' I caught hold of her skirt. 'If you should slip—' But I crowded closer, too, keeping one hand firmly on the door jamb.

It was a long way down. Three floors—and voices carried. I tried, but it wasn't quite possible to pinpoint the floor the voices were coming from. They seemed to rise from nowhere and echo everywhere. We didn't even know who occupied the other apartments abutting on the blank echoing space.

'I HATE YOU!' a voice boomed with sudden destructive clarity and the words rebounded across the empty air. 'Hate you . . . hate you . . . hate you . . .'

'Party's getting rough,' I murmured, with more insouciance than I felt. Someone was getting desperate down there. Violence quivered through the great echoing well.

'I'll see you in hell!' the other snarled back. 'The sooner, the better!'

Why were the voices suddenly so loud and clear? I was abruptly aware of the arrow of light shining across the space from our partly-opened door. If a corresponding door had opened below us, surely there would be more light reaching out across the darkness.

'Please—' a female voice intervened. Where had she come from? Had she been there all along?

'Please . . . we won't get anywhere this way. We've been over this before . . .' The voices began to fade again. They must be moving away from the door.

Someone said something completely inaudible and I had just decided the show was over when an almighty crash sent us both leaping back from the door.

'I'LL KILL YOU FOR THAT!' a voice bellowed. Then there was silence.

We waited, but there were no further sounds.

'Well, well, well.' Evangeline closed the door and leaned against it thoughtfully. 'It appears that we have our own whispering gallery.'

'Where was it coming from? Could you tell?'

'From one of the flats immediately below us. Or possibly from the staircase. Nothing appears to be soundproofed in this place and the way the voices faded in would tally with the way stairs level off at landings, then the voices faded out again as people turned to descend the next flight of stairs.'

'You mean they were having a fight all the way down the stairs? Maybe—' It fitted. 'Maybe that's what that awful crash was—somebody pushed somebody else down the stairs. They were certainly furious enough.'

I had a sudden thought and started across the kitchen. 'Maybe they're still on the stairs. If we hurry, we can find out who they are.'

'Pause and reflect, Trixie.' Evangeline moved the chair back in front of the door. 'Do you really want to encounter a group of people in the mood they're in?'

I hesitated. She had a point. Besides, they were probably on the ground floor by now. If they'd been on the stairs to begin with. It was far more likely that we had tuned in on a fight in one of the flats.

'I'd say the mood was murderous,' Evangeline suggested softly. 'And we've had enough of that.'

CHAPTER 5

Morning was wild, wet and windy. A hurricane and a half was howling around outside. I felt as though I was trapped in an action replay of the past few weeks—except that we were within taxiing distance of the centre of London.

On the other hand, life had been very hectic recently and the prospect of a day just lounging around with our feet up was rather tempting. I had picked up a selection of magazines and paperbacks with the rest of the shopping last night.

When I skirted the drawing-room on the way to the kitchen, I saw that Evangeline had had the same idea. She was propped up on the sofa with a cup of coffee, one of the large luscious Danish pastries I had not been able to resist buying and the copies of the *Tatler* and *Harpers & Queen*.

'I think a quiet day is long overdue,' she informed me.

'How true, how true.' She'd get no argument from me on that one. I foraged for my own coffee and Danish and

rejoined her, curling up in the big armchair with the magazines she had already discarded.

Peace—it was wonderful. For a long while, the only
sounds were the wind and the beating of rain on the
windows and pages turning.

Then the telephone rang.

'Don't answer it,' Evangeline said. 'Pretend we're not
here.'

But someone knew better. The phone rang and rang,
obviously intent on waking us if we were still asleep. They
weren't going to give up easily. The ringing was beginning
to get on my nerves—that was what they were counting
on.

Naturally, it stopped ringing just as I picked it up.

'There you are.' Evangeline grimaced her sympathy. 'No
stamina. Never mind, if it's really important, they'll call
back.'

'Next time it rings—' I gave the phone a disgusted
look—'maybe I *won't* answer it.'

'Maybe . . .' Evangeline yawned and let her magazine
slip to the floor. 'These lazy days are all very well, but we
ought to take *some* exercise.'

'Really?' I looked pointedly at the rain still battering our
windows. 'What did you have in mind?' I couldn't really
visualize Evangeline climbing into a leotard and joining me
in a workout.

'I thought . . .' She widened her eyes in elaborate innocence. 'I thought it might be nice just to take a gentle
stroll through the building. You know, up and down the
corridors, from floor to floor, using the stairs going down
and taking the elevator back up from the lobby. It would
help us to get our bearings in relation to the other flats, see
where people live, that sort of thing.'

Snooping, she meant. Still, it wasn't a bad idea. And it
would provide some exercise.

'Then, when we come back, we can have lunch—and feel we've earned it.' Sensing that I was weakening, she pressed her case. 'Didn't I see a quiche in last night's shopping?'

'Chicken and asparagus,' I admitted. 'And I got a carton of watercress soup.'

'Splendid! A luncheon fit for the gods.' She was laying it on with a trowel; I began to suspect that she might have more mischief in mind than I already suspected.

'I'll just go and get into my shoes, these slippers are a bit too informal in case we meet anyone. Oh, and Trixie, I think we should wear those nice black merino shawls Job let us keep as a souvenir of the film. The corridors might be draughty . . .'

She went directly to the secret—well, concealed—door and pressed exactly the right spot on the panel. Of course, I could have done that myself; I was paying just as much attention as she was when the secret had been revealed. You never know when knowing a thing like that might come in handy.

The panel swung closed behind us and we had to stand there for a minute to let our eyes become accustomed to the gloom. Oh, there was safety lighting—I'm sure the law required it—but the wattage was the lowest it was possible to get without using actual candles. I'll bet the law visualized something better than that for Fire Stairs.

'Jasper must have got a good price on a job lot of 20-watt bulbs,' Evangeline grumbled as we started down the stairs. 'There's a lot of his grandfather in that boy.'

'Why do we always get stuck with the cheapskates?'

'Oh, we've run across a few in our time who weren't so tight with their money.' Evangeline gave an unexpected girlish giggle. 'Those were the ones we married.'

'True.' The memory of my first ranch mink coat being

spread across the foot of the bed on a first wedding anniversary brought a smile to my face. 'But I don't envy the girl who marries Jasper—she's got a lot of retraining to do.'

'That's her problem.' We had reached the floor below and Evangeline flung open the door with reckless disregard for anyone who might be passing.

Fortunately, the corridor was deserted—and it *was* a corridor, not a foyer as on the penthouse floor. This floor, and probably all the lower floors, had been carved up into more flats. There were three doors on each side of the corridor, indicating smaller flats.

In fact, I glanced upwards and made a quick calculation as to where we were in relation to our penthouse suite: at least one of the doors was nothing more than a false promise. It would open into that vast echoing space where more apartments were yet to be built.

'No, Evangeline,' I said, as she reached out a hand to the doorknob. 'If it isn't locked, we don't want to know about it.'

'Yes, we do.' She tested it and seemed disappointed to find it locked. 'For Beau's sake, we must try to watch over Jasper.' She sighed dramatically. 'I feel as though I am *in loco parentis* to that boy.'

'Only the *loco* is right,' I muttered.

She sniffed and moved back towards the stairs. It suited me; there wasn't much to see in this corridor and I had already noted that no one we had already met was behind the numbering on these doors.

Mindful of the quarrel we had overheard, I looked closely at the walls of the staircase, but there was no sign of violence on them. Perhaps it had sounded worse than it actually was.

The next floor down also had three doors on each side; but, again, one of them must be for an apartment that didn't exist.

I wondered suddenly just how many doors on the other side of the corridor opened on to blank space. Our side was the one with the river views; therefore, the most desirable. Surely they'd have finished all the apartments on that side first—if they could. I was swept by the eerie feeling that the penthouse was like the crow's nest of an old sailing ship—perhaps one of the very ships that had once unloaded cargo at our wharf. We were perched precariously at the top of a long high mast with emptiness stretching endlessly below us.

'If I'm correct—' Evangeline had no doubt about it. 'I believe Nigel has one of these apartments. I wonder which one.'

'Just follow your nose.' There was a faint smell of burnt food in the air, growing stronger as we neared the corner flat. 'I don't know why that man keeps trying to cook when he has such terrible results.'

'Perhaps he can't master the high-tech kitchen apparatus.' For Evangeline, it was a charitable statement, then she ruined it. 'And he's too stupid to give up.'

'According to Roz, Jasper thinks he's a financial genius. I suppose you can't be talented at everything.' And I had the clear impression that Nigel cared more about money than he did about food.

'That may explain a lot about Jasper's financial situation. The boy has no judgement at all. If Nigel is such a genius, why hasn't he got a job? He doesn't fool *me* with all that talk about his own consultancy and working from home. That man is "resting" as surely as any out-of-work actor I ever met.'

'You know . . .' It hadn't occurred to me before. 'I think you're right.'

'You needn't sound so surprised about it. I'm usually right.' She was definitely mellowing. Time was when she'd have claimed she was always right.

'We're resting ourselves,' I reminded her.

'But from choice. And not for long. Just for a week or so while we recover from the rigours of Whitby.'

We re-entered the stairwell and went down to explore the next floor, where I mentally noted the location of The Chummery. After that, the remaining floors were very dull, containing more flats, but no familiar numbers. By the time we had reached the floor just above the lobby, we had a pretty good idea of the layout of the building. The penthouse had the largest apartments, the three floors immediately below had smaller, but still sizeable, flats and the next three had flats of varying size, with the smaller facing the river, obviously trading size for the luxury of a river view.

This floor was different; the corridor was spacious and open at one end with an arrangement of mismatched armchairs and a sofa, floor lamps and coffee table holding several magazines and a flower arrangement. Against the back wall was a bookcase filled with recently published hardbacks and paperbacks. It seemed to be an upper lobby, less informal and quite comfortable, a gathering place for the residents. As we strolled closer, we saw a sofa table behind the sofa holding an elaborate clock which chimed the half-hour as we approached.

'How charming,' I said. 'It's like a room without walls.'

'Or a stage set.' Evangeline regarded it critically, then sat in one of the armchairs, drawing her shawl around her.

'It's nice, though.' I took one of the other armchairs. 'Like a club room. Maybe that's what they had in mind. One floor for a general gathering place with amenities, so that it's like living in a very exclusive residential hotel. You have your own quarters, but you can come down here if you're feeling social and mingle with other residents who feel like companionship. It's a good idea.'

'It always was.' Evangeline had lived in a few of these self-sufficient apartment blocks herself in the States. 'Too bad Jasper hasn't been able to follow through properly on it. There obviously ought to be a gymnasium there—' She gestured to one side of the wide corridor. 'And a restaurant there on the river side, where customers can enjoy the view as they dine.'

'The underground garage hasn't been built yet, either.' I, too, had read the prospectus we had found casually displayed on the coffee table in the penthouse. 'I suppose it would have been so fiendishly expensive he decided to wait until he'd sold most of the leases and then finance it from the proceeds.'

'Shhhh!' Evangeline gestured sharply, then tilted her head listening—but not to me. 'There's someone in there.'

'Why shouldn't there be?'

But Evangeline was already on her feet and heading for one of the doors opening on to the river side. She tapped on the door with one hand and tried the knob with the other. The door swung open and she stepped inside. I followed her, mouth still open to protest.

'I'm sorry.' A young woman moved forward swiftly to block her path. 'We're not open.'

'Oh?' Evangeline paused and we both looked around. In front of a curtain partitioning off the far end of the room there was a cluster of wooden tables with chairs piled upside down on them.

'We've just moved into one of the penthouse suites,' Evangeline said. 'We were given to understand that there was a restaurant on the premises.'

'That's right, there is.' The woman looked faintly embarrassed. 'That is, there will be. But we're not open yet.'

'I see.' Evangeline swept the long narrow empty room with an insulting glance. 'And just when do you plan to open? This year . . . next year . . . ?'

Sometime . . . never . . . ? hung in the air. The young woman flushed a deep red.

'Soon!' she blurted out. 'Very soon. Meanwhile, we're serving Sunday Leisurely Luncheons on *The Gliding Gourmet*, from one-thirty to four-thirty p.m. Or later, we don't rush you. You'll have to book if you want to come. We only have just so many covers.'

'*This*,' Evangeline pointed out severely, 'happens to be Thursday—and we are hungry.'

'I'm sorry.' The curtain at the far end of the room moved and a man came out from behind it and walked forward to join us. The curtain fell back into place—but not before I had seen the bed behind it. So they were camping out in their long, echoing restaurant-to-be. At that, it was probably warmer than sleeping aboard the boat in this weather.

'I'm sorry, but that has to be the best offer at the moment.' The man smiled at Evangeline. 'In another week or ten days, we'll have this place in shape and we'll be doing dinners every night—although possibly not lunches, at first.'

'You're sure?' Evangeline looked around in open disbelief.

'Oh yes,' the young woman said. 'Now that we have a new backer—' She broke off as her partner nudged her.

'I'm glad to hear that.' Evangeline switched into gracious mode. 'It will be so convenient to have a restaurant in the building.' She spoke as though we were going to be permanent residents.

'Meanwhile,' I put in quickly, 'we'll book a table for the Leisurely Luncheon for Sunday on *The Gliding Gourmet*.' It wouldn't do any harm to check out just how good the cooking was before we got too enthusiastic about their restaurant.

'We're not licensed,' the man said, 'so feel free to bring your own bottle. Everyone does. There's no corkage charge.'

'The tables are for four,' the girl said. 'Will you be bringing guests, or do you want to share a table?'

'*Share?*' Evangeline gave her a look to freeze the marrow
in her bones. 'We will bring guests, of course.'

It was the first I'd heard of it. I could understand that
a struggling restaurant wouldn't want to waste two reservations on their busiest day—in fact, their only day—of
the week. I also knew that Evangeline would rather sink
the boat than share a table with strangers.

But who did she have in mind for guests? Martha and
Hugh were still on their prolonged honeymoon; Gwenda,
Des and Julian were still up in Whitby working on retakes
for the film; and practically anyone else I could think of
was a non-starter. I glanced at her curiously. Someone from
her past? From the days when she had starred in the West
End with any number of now-famous colleagues?

'Do you have a card?' Evangeline asked.

'Oh, sorry, yes.' He pulled one from his pocket and
handed it to her.

'*The Gliding Gourmet* . . .' Evangeline read, holding it at
a fastidious distance. It was dog-eared, grubby, and had
obviously seen better days. 'And you, I take it, are "Sophie
& Frederick Morton, Proprietors"?'

'The same.' It was obvious that they had seen better
days, too. Although, if they had a new backer, they were
on their way up again.

'We'll be having new cards printed for the opening,'
Frederick said. 'I hope you'll come.'

'That will depend on our commitments—'

'Of course, Miss Sinclair. I realize you and Miss Dolan
must be very busy.'

'But we shall try.' Evangeline smiled in satisfaction. That
was better, she *had* been recognized and the proper defer-
ence was being shown.

Other than that, I could tell that boredom was setting

in. They were nice people and their food was probably good, but they were no 'Prince' Mike Romanov or Sherman Billingsley. The flamboyant restaurateurs of Hollywood and New York had been a bigger draw than some of the *artistes* in their floor shows—and often provided better entertainment. They had spoiled us for less charismatic proprietors.

'Well . . .' Evangeline began moving towards the door. As though mesmerized, the Mortons moved along with her. Frederick leaped to open the door for her.

'Remember, you never heard this from me—' The voice, as most portentously-lowered voices are apt to do, carried farther than a normal tone would have done. 'And, on my oath, I never heard it from the person who told it to me, but . . .'

By this time, we had all moved out into the upper lobby and could see Nigel lounging in one of the armchairs, his ubiquitous telephone clutched close to his mouth.

'In a position to know, yes . . .' He listened for a moment; he hadn't noticed us yet. 'That's what they were supposed to think. He's been back in the country for several days now. Not looking at all well. Of course, at his age . . . not unexpected. I heard . . . as a doornail, old man.'

There was a gasp and a thud behind us. I turned to find that Sophie had slumped to the floor in a dead faint.

'It's all right, I've got her.' Frederick stopped and gathered her up. 'Don't worry, she does this occasionally. I'll see to her.' He was obviously anxious to forestall any attempt to help.

'If you're *quite* sure . . .' He needn't have bothered so far as Evangeline was concerned; she had no intention of offering to help. And I had already seen the bed concealed behind the curtain, although he didn't realize that.

'Oh, quite. Quite.' He was backing into the shell of the restaurant with her, grimacing extravagantly to show how

casual he was. 'She's very delicate, that's all. A glass of
water and a bit of a lie-down and she'll be fine.' The door
closed behind them.

That left us free to concentrate on more important
matters.

'And now—' Evangeline swept forward, pinning Nigel
with a sharp look—'just *who* has died?'

CHAPTER 6

'Died? Died?' Nigel tried to brazen it out. 'I don't know
what you're talking about.'

'Oh, come now.' Evangeline gave him no quarter. 'You
distinctly said, "as a doornail". I've never heard anyone
referred to as healthy as a doornail.'

I nodded agreement, for what it was worth.

'Oh, *that!*' Nigel looked at us critically, as though trying
to decide what we'd believe.

'I was just—' *Practically anything* must have been the
answer. 'I was just telling a colleague about a new share
issue. A real no-hoper. Dead as a doornail. You should have
seen the prospectus. A baby wouldn't have fallen for it.'

And did *he* really think *we* were going to fall for *that?* We
didn't even bother to exchange glances. It would have taken
more than a dud share issue to make young Sophie collapse
in a heap.

'How interesting,' Evangeline said flatly.

'Ah well, perhaps not,' Nigel acknowledged. 'Not unless
you're personally involved.'

Precisely. So why had Sophie fainted? Unless she found
herself faced with the loss of a backer who had been about
to bankroll them out of their problems. Come to think of
it, Frederick had looked pretty ashen-faced himself.

'What are you ladies doing down here?' Nigel decided to take the offensive. 'The restaurant isn't open yet.'

'So we discovered,' Evangeline said.

'We decided to take a little exercise,' I explained. 'It's too wet to go outside, so we thought we'd stroll around the corridors.'

'Ah! Like taking a turn around the deck on board ship, eh?'

'That's it. Except that you don't see so many people. In fact, no one at all until we got down here.'

'Ah! Yes! Busy place here.' He waved his hand, indicating the room setting. 'Sort of a gathering spot. Or will be when it's fixed up a bit more. And there are more people. It's busier in the evenings.'

'Of course. When people come home from work.' Evangeline looked at him pointedly.

'Don't you believe it! Most of them are out job-hunting. Those of us—' he waggled his cellphone at her—'who can work from home are the lucky ones.

'Mind you . . .' He grew wistful. 'I must admit I miss the old push-and-shove hubbub of the Stock Exchange floor in the good old days. One gets such a sense of isolation now. Anywhere you can connect a computer terminal is an office. It's not the same at all.'

'Nothing ever is,' Evangeline sympathized. 'And things can change so fast . . .'

'That's true. I'm still a young man, but when I think of the changes I've seen in just the past few years, I feel a hundred years old.'

'Yes,' Evangeline said softly, 'and I've seen even more. New inventions making old methods obsolete almost overnight . . . familiar products replaced by "improved" versions, which never are . . . Stock Markets crashing . . .'

'Companies failing,' Nigel joined in; she seemed to be

having an almost hypnotic effect on him. 'Whole depart-
ments wiped out . . . jobs lost . . .'

'People dying . . .' Her voice was a soft coo, inviting con-
fidences.

'Ah!' He recoiled and glared at her. She'd nearly had
him, but he'd recovered himself in time.

'Ah well . . .' He looked at his watch. 'Must be off. See
you again no doubt . . .'

'That young man,' Evangeline said darkly as he vanished
into the lift, 'is up to no good.'

'That wouldn't surprise me.' Very little would. 'Who do
you think is dead? And why doesn't he want us to know?'

'Just what I was wondering.' She cocked her head towards the burst of wild sobbing coming from behind the
door. 'It sounds as though someone knows the answer—
or thinks she does.' She paused before continuing wistfully.
'I suppose we really couldn't knock on the door and offer
help?'

'No, we couldn't!' Enough was enough, although I'd have
liked to know the answers myself. 'Not right now, anyway.
I don't know about you, but I'm ready for lunch.'

'If you can heat it up without blasting us off to Mars.'
She followed me meekly down what seemed to be the Grand
Staircase to the lobby and over to the elevators.

'We can check out the lobby any old time.' I looked
around. 'There's not much to it.'

'Shells! Empty shells! Just like the propped-up shopfronts
in an El Cheapo western.' Evangeline snorted. 'What will
you bet that not even the caretaker's flat is completed?'

'Nothing. Why should it be? They haven't got a caretaker, either.'

'Quite right. This place doesn't run to such luxuries. If
they had one, Roz wouldn't have been ringing Jasper's bell
to complain about her heating.'

'If you believe that.' I didn't.

'Not for an instant. She's up to something, too.' Evangeline's eyes narrowed. 'And so is Jasper. Especially Jasper. We must try to get him into a reasonable frame of mind and insist that he retains a caretaker. Otherwise . . .'

'Otherwise . . . if anything breaks down, we have to call on *Jasper?*' I closed my eyes, trying not to contemplate it. Jasper was a dear boy but, on any list of people I would be willing to call on in a mechanical emergency, he ranked somewhere below the head of the local bird-watching society and the star of the kindergarten finger-painting class.

'You're beginning to grasp the problem.' The lift doors slid open and Evangeline marched into it. I followed numbly.

'On the other hand—' Evangeline began to cheer up. 'It may not be that bad. This *is* a very recent modernization and there shouldn't be much that could go wrong . . .'

A nasty whine reverberated through the lift shaft and the lights dimmed.

'It looks like the guarantee is running out already,' I said, hoping I hadn't gone as pale as she had.

The lift quivered, but continued upwards—at about one-tenth of its usual speed. I held my breath. Evangeline's eyes widened and she didn't seem to be breathing, either.

Slowly the lift crawled level with the next floor, then put on a spurt of speed and lurched past it before we had time to push the OPEN DOOR button. Someone whimpered softly and I was afraid that it was me.

'Steady, Trixie!' Evangeline reached out a hand which would have been comforting if it hadn't been shaking so much.

'It's OK.' It wasn't and we both knew it. We clutched hands and stood motionless, *willing* the power not to fail. The light was a mere glimmer and a snail would have looked like an Olympic Gold compared to our pace.

'Before it gives up entirely—' Evangeline leaned over and stabbed at the red EMERGENCY button. Nothing seemed to happen.

'It's probably ringing in the caretaker's flat,' I said despairingly.

'Only too likely, I'm afraid.' Evangeline jabbed at it again and again. We didn't hear a sound.

'People will come . . . eventually.' I tried to close out the mental image of Olivia de Havilland trapped between floors for an entire weekend in *Lady in a Lift*.

'I wouldn't like to bet on that.' Evangeline was grim-faced.

I decided to concentrate on the de Havilland movie's inspirational aspects. At least, the lift *stayed* where it had stopped. It didn't go plunging down—

There was a deep hum from somewhere below us, gradually growing louder and closer. I recognized it as the sister-lift, the stop-at-every-floor local Jason had been so scathing about. It drew abreast of us and soared effortlessly past us.

'HELP!' I shrieked as I judged it was passing. 'HELP! We're stuck! Get us out of here!'

For an awful moment there was no response. I began to wonder if the lifts were the only thing in the building soundproofed.

'All right . . . Don't worry . . .' At last, the echoing, fading-upwards answer came. 'You're still moving . . . you'll get there . . .'

'It's Frederick and Sophie,' Evangeline said. 'What are they doing, going up to the penthouse?'

'We'll wind you down,' Sophie shouted. 'We've watched the Fire Brigade do it. If you stop . . . we'll wind you down.'

'The Fire Brigade again?' Evangeline was nearly as mistrustful as I was. 'What have they to do with it? Has this sort of thing happened before?'

'It sounds like a regular occurrence,' I said. 'We seem

to be the only suckers who don't know about it.' I looked through the little glass panel and saw that the view outside kept shifting gradually. 'We're still moving, anyway.'

'Are you sure?' There was a judder and the floor seemed to sink a few inches. We both screamed.

'Are you all right down there?' There was a note of panic in Frederick's voice.

'We're sinking!' Evangeline shrieked. 'And there aren't any lifeboats!'

'It's all right, it's all right.' Frederick's voice was placating. 'It always does that at the sixth floor. That's good. It means you're almost here.'

Slowly, grudgingly, the upward progress began again.

'I'm going to kill Jasper,' Evangeline said between clenched teeth. 'How dare he put us into a situation like this?'

'And with no warning.' I was in total agreement. 'This place is full of traps for the unwary.'

'That's it. You're doing well.' Both voices had shifted into encouraging tones. 'You're going to make it.'

'I'd like that in writing,' Evangeline muttered. 'With a money-back guarantee.'

'I didn't say anything. I was too busy holding my breath.

Evangeline gave a muffled shriek, but it was only because two pale grimacing faces had come into view outside the little glass panel.

'Nearly there. We'll meet you upstairs,' they called, pointing vigorously upwards.

'They have more faith than I have,' Evangeline said.

I risked taking a deep breath and nodded.

After an eternity-and-a-half, the lift juddered to a stop again, shimmied indecisively for a few decades, then abruptly released the doors, snapping them open without warning.

We stumbled into the foyer, having been leaning against the doors in order to better pry them apart.

'Are you all right?' Frederick asked.

'Brandy!' Evangeline gasped.

'Of course, but I'm afraid I'll have to go downstairs to get some. Just hang on—'

'No, in here.' Evangeline began scrabbling at the lock of our door with the key.

'Won't you join us?' I wasn't just being polite. Sophie looked as though she needed a restorative more than we did—and that was saying something.

'No. Oh no!' Sophie recoiled. 'I mean, thank you, but—but we must speak to—' Her voice trembled.

'We came up to call on your neighbour,' Frederick said. 'Now, if you'll excuse us . . .' He turned away and rang the bell of the next-door corner penthouse.

His tone had been casual, but his mask slipped as they waited for someone to answer. For a split second his face wore the same expression of desperate urgency as Sophie's.

'I'm not sure there's anyone there.' I tried to break it to them gently. 'We never hear a sound from there. I didn't realize it was occupied.'

Sophie gave a stifled sob and bit at her knuckle. Frederick put a steadying hand on her shoulder.

Evangeline had our door open now but, scenting drama, had changed her mind about going in. She loitered shamelessly in the doorway, waiting to see what was going to happen.

'Ring again,' she urged. 'The doorbells may not be in any better shape than the elevator.'

Frederick's lips tightened, but he pressed the bell again. This time we could hear it ring sharply.

This time, too, it was Sophie who was holding her breath. Both of them looked as though they were facing the end of the world.

'Yes! Yes! What is it?' The door was flung open and a short chunky man stood glaring out at us.

'Sorry to disturb you—' Frederick seemed frightened, now that he had found the person he was looking for. 'But we wanted to be sure you were all right.'

'All right? All right? Why shouldn't I be all right?' The man was not in a good temper. I was glad I wasn't the one who had disturbed him.

'You're alive . . .' Sophie breathed a deep sigh and slumped to the floor.

'There she goes again.' Evangeline looked down at her critically. 'Anæmic, if you ask me. She needs vitamin supplements.'

'Why?' The man's voice was soft with menace. 'Why shouldn't I be alive? What is she talking about?'

'There was a rumour . . .' Frederick struggled to lift Sophie to her feet. 'A wild rumour going around that . . .'

'Rumour? Rumour? Who is spreading such a rumour?'

'I, er . . . I couldn't say. It seems to be everywhere.' Frederick had Sophie in his arms now and was looking around uncomfortably.

'Bring her in here,' the man ordered.

'We'll take her,' Evangeline countermanded. 'She can lie down and have a brandy.'

Frederick looked from one to the other, as though he were being asked to choose between the lady or the tiger— and wasn't sure which had the sharper teeth.

'I'll take her downstairs.' Frederick headed for the lift. 'She can rest there.'

'Not if you use *that* lift,' I reminded him as he started to step into the alleged 'Express'.

'Oh yes.' He backed out hastily and moved over to the 'Local'.

I watched the doors close behind them, then turned to

find Evangeline and our neighbour eyeing each other assessingly.

'I have seen you before, I think,' our neighbour said. 'But not here.'

'I was thinking the same about you,' Evangeline responded. 'Are you a film fan?'

'I have no time these days, but once it was my only escape. Yes, yes, I know you now.' He turned to me. 'And you, also. Forgive my slowness.'

'I gather you're someone in the financial field,' Evangeline said. 'Possibly with a company or two quoted on the Stock Market?'

'Lazlo Tronnix, at your service. My company, Multitronics International, began as a small purveyor of electronic equipment I invented myself, but has grown into what is now called a conglomerate with branches all over the world. It is quoted on many Stock Exchanges.'

'And am I right in thinking—' Evangeline met his eyes—'that those Stock Exchanges would be in some disarray if the news of your sudden death were to reach them?'

'There would be international repercussions, yes.' He got the message. 'And rumours are being spread. This happens periodically to one or another of us. It is an attempt to manipulate the market.' He was wearing an expression I'd hate to see coming towards me down a dark alley. 'It will be dealt with.'

'I'm sure it will,' Evangeline said drily.

'Now, if you will excuse me, I must begin issuing faxes and making telephone calls to let people know I am still alive.'

'Electronics are all very well,' Evangeline said, 'but, personally speaking, on the occasion or two when this has happened to me, I've found the best thing to do is dress up and go out on the town. Let everyone see you in action and they'll have no doubts.'

'Wise, as well as beautiful.' He nodded several times. 'In that case, ladies, may I offer you dinner tonight at the Savoy? With two such companions, the world will indeed be sure that I am alive—and kicking. My car will be here at eight.'

'We might make a gossip column or two,' Evangeline said modestly, while I began planning what to wear. Plenty of glitz and glamour was definitely called for.

'If I might make a further suggestion,' Evangeline continued. 'Have the car here at seven, or even six-thirty. We can stop for champagne at one or two of the watering-holes where your appearance will do the most good. It will start the word spreading faster than waiting for the morning papers.'

'The brilliance! The deviousness! We will do that!' He looked at her sharply for a moment. 'I don't suppose you would consider joining my Board of Directors?'

'Mmm . . .' She was tempted, I could tell. 'Perhaps not, but thank you. I have too many other commitments.'

'Naturally. You must be in great demand.' He sketched a bow. 'Then I will call for you at six-thirty. There is a certain bar in the City that will be crowded with insiders at that hour. What an entrance we will make!'

'You can count on it,' she promised.

'Well,' I said, as we withdrew behind our respective doors and closed them behind us, 'I have the feeling that you've just put a great big spoke in Nigel's wheeler-dealering.'

'I certainly hope so,' she said.

CHAPTER 7

Who says you can't get a hangover from champagne? You can get a hangover from carrot juice, if you drink enough of it—and furthermore, your skin turns bright orange. That seemed to be the only thing I was spared this morning.

After turning away from my mirror, I tottered into the kitchen and collected a cup of coffee. The percolator was half-empty and still hot, so I knew Evangeline was up and around somewhere. I drank one cup standing there, then poured another and carried it into the drawing-room.

Evangeline was collapsed on the sofa, a boneless wreck, with only enough strength to lift the black coffee to her trembling lips. Her eyes were closed. I knew just how she felt.

'Evangeline,' I pleaded faintly, 'tell me I didn't do the Shimmy on a tabletop last night.'

'Sure.' She opened one eye. 'If you'll tell me I wasn't doing the Charleston on an adjoining table.' She took a sip of coffee and opened the other eye, meeting mine.

'And then make me believe it!' we chorused.

'It's all right,' Evangeline said. 'We moved down to the dance floor for the encore. Lazlo was right there with us.'

'So was half the town.' It was beginning to come back to me. We had hit about four very exclusive watering-places in the City, picking up an assortment of brokers and bankers in each. Mostly, they had seemed to be staid and fairly elderly gentlemen, who had grown younger and wilder as the evening wore on and the champagne flowed like the Thames.

'You and Lazlo did a fantastic exhibition of jitterbugging.' Evangeline was beginning to perk up. 'The photogra-

phers were following us around by then, so you might have
made some of the papers.'

'Jitterbugging?' I squeaked. 'In that long slim skirt I was
wearing?'

'Don't worry,' Evangeline said. 'It split right along the
seam and looked as though it was supposed to be that way.
Long split skirts are all the rage now. Especially thigh-high
splits.'

I moaned faintly. Jitterbugging. No wonder I ached in
every bone and muscle this morning. Obviously, I couldn't
blame everything on the champagne. But I doubted I'd
have been jitterbugging without it.

'Everyone was terribly impressed when Lazlo threw you
over his shoulder and swung you around. I think myself he
got a touch of French Apache mixed in with the jitterbugging, but no one else was old enough to know better—well,
very few. Lazlo said he learned it from the GI's after the
War.'

'I wish I'd been old enough to know better.' I stared
gloomily at a bruise I had just discovered on my forearm.
It seemed to be the size and shape of spread fingers. I
wondered where else I might find such bruises—and decided I wasn't going to have enough courage to look.

That was when the doorbell rang. I staggered over to
open the door and found myself gazing at a small forest. I
blinked and it turned into a four-foot orange tree, complete
with oranges in various stages of ripeness.

'Miss Dolan?' A voice spoke from behind the tree.

'Yes,' I admitted, stepping back. He lurched past me
and deposited the tree in the middle of the drawing-room.

'Miss Sinclair?' There was another of them standing in
the doorway. A delivery boy, I mean. This one was carrying
a flower arrangement that dwarfed him. He carried it over
and set it beside the sofa before Evangeline had time to
answer.

'Sign here, please.' Both of them flourished autograph books instead of delivery receipts.

'Your pictures are in all the papers,' one of them said as we obliged. 'You looked great.' The other nudged him sharply. 'You still do. What a wild night, eh?'

The other nudged him again and they both left quickly.

I opened the square white envelope I found attached to a lower branch: '*To keep you from being homesick until we can set up our own little Nest in the West. Love, your Bobbikins.*' I winced.

'Who the hell is my Bobbikins?'

'Search me.' Evangeline had problems of her own. 'Who is Roger, my would-be Lodger?'

The doorbell rang again as we were mulling over these vital questions. This time there was a procession of delivery people bearing bouquets, boxes of chocolates and magnums of champagne.

'Stage-Door Johnnies still exist,' Evangeline said complacently. 'Apparently we gave a lot of men their youth back last night.'

'I just hope their wives appreciate it.'

The doorbell rang again. 'Why do I bother to close the door? I might just as well leave it open today. Come one, come all—oh, good morning, Lazlo.'

'A beautiful morning, a divine morning.' He waltzed into the room, dropping a double kiss on my cheeks as he passed and went on to do the same to Evangeline.

'Have you seen the newspapers this morning?' He was carrying a stack of them. 'We made every front page in town. Tomorrow it will be the Continent, the States—' He waved the top tabloid enthusiastically before my eyes.

The picture took up half the front page; the headlines the rest. A beaming Lazlo was bent double, holding someone whose hair swept the floor. A pair of long, still shapely legs flailed out from under his armpits. I knew with dreadful certainty that they were mine.

'Does every paper have that same picture?' I asked weakly. I supposed I hadn't a snowball in hell's chance that Martha wouldn't see it somewhere.

'Some of them are even better!' Lazlo was gleeful. 'Already Multitronics has gained fifty-three pence on the Stock Market. That regains the twenty it dropped at closing last night, when the death rumours were circulating, and thirty-three above that. And still rising!'

'Congratulations,' Evangeline said coldly. 'It's nice to know that one's labours have not been in vain.'

'But look! You can see for yourselves.' He handed each of us a pile of papers, holding them oddly.

'Sit down,' he insisted, before giving me mine.

Since it was what I had in mind anyway, I sat and accepted my papers. A small flat box slithered out of the midst of the papers and into my lap. A jeweller's box. Looking across, I saw that Evangeline had one, too.

'Lazlo, darling, you shouldn't have!' she cooed, opening it and taking out something bright and glittering.

'No, you shouldn't have,' I echoed, opening my own. 'Oooooh, but I'm glad that you did. It's beautiful!' I held aloft the shimmering brooch, a trembler waterfall of tiny diamonds spraying up from a large opal fountain.

Still cooing, Evangeline and I exchanged brooches for mutual admiration. Hers was also a trembler waterfall of diamonds, but from a black fire opal fountain. I wondered if the brooches had been meant as a pair—and who Lazlo had bought them for originally. We exchanged glances as we each took our own brooch back and I knew Evangeline was wondering the same thing.

'Oh, wait a minute!' I had a sudden thought and dashed for my handbag to fish out a penny—fortunately, a bright and shining one.

'Here—' I thrust it at Lazlo, who looked puzzled. 'Because there's a sharp point on the fastening pin,' I explained. 'You have to give the giver a penny when something is sharp—so that it doesn't cut the friendship.'

'That's right.' Evangeline was already delving into her own bag. We didn't want to risk a break-up with anyone who gave away such splendiferous jewellery.

'You are superstitious then?' Lazlo looked disappointed. 'Perhaps you also believe that opals bring bad luck. Some people do.' His face darkened and I wondered if that was why he'd had the brooches; she'd refused them because of the opals. 'Shall I take them back and get you something else?'

'Oh no! They're beautiful! They could never be unlucky.' I quickly pinned my brooch on. It had never, ever, occurred to me to associate bad luck with jewellery. I wouldn't even turn down the Hope Diamond.

'That's right,' Evangeline said. 'The superstition about opals arose because they have a tendency to shrink slightly and sometimes drop out of their settings. When enough people had noticed that their opal had disappeared, they began to think opals were bad luck because they were so easily lost. If you just keep an eye on your setting and make sure it's tight, you'll never have any trouble with an opal. This seems nice and firm.'

Leave it to Evangeline to know the most esoteric facts about gemstones. If it sparkled, she was an expert on it.

'The settings have been strengthened.' Lazlo nodded. 'Otherwise, they are the same. Only a vandal would have changed anything about them. They are unique.'

'Works of art,' I agreed happily.

'A fountain by night and by day . . .' Evangeline was admiring hers again. 'Sunshine and shadow . . .' She sounded quite satisfied to be thought of as night and shadow.

'A mere downpayment.' Lazlo waved his hand dismissively. 'I owe you much. It is not that my company would have crashed,' he added quickly, just in case we might think he owed us *too* much, 'but you have saved me much time and work by helping to prove all rumours false before they spread too widely.'

'It was almost a pleasure.' Evangeline touched her forehead lightly and winced.

'Really, you don't owe us anything—' I broke off as Evangeline shot me a look that could have cracked marble.

'I pay my debts.' He brushed aside both our comments and his face hardened unpleasantly. 'And I do not forget what I owe to the person who began these rumours and to those who spread them.'

I was suddenly very glad that I hadn't mentioned Nigel. If Lazlo found out, it wasn't going to be from me. Whatever happened to Nigel wasn't going to be on my conscience.

Even as I repressed a shudder, I wondered where that thought had come from. Lazlo had never been anything but charming, gracious and appreciative to us. Why, then, should I suddenly visualize dark unlit alleys, furtive footsteps, deep shadows that separated to become human forms waiting in ambush? A faint scent of an exotic foreign tobacco . . . ?

Of course! *Vengeance in Vienna*, when I played the cabaret singer who, just as the war was ending, got mixed up with an SS deserter who was pretending to have been anti-Hitler all along, but was really only interested in setting up a new black market and had begun by blackmailing the cabaret owner into claiming him as a brother and hiding him during the last days of the bombing. (Our nightclub was conveniently in a cellar anyway.) I'd been half in love with the nightclub owner, but he'd been acting strangely under the stress of bombings and blackmail and, once the first of the GI Joes marched into town, I realized the error of my ways. My ex-lover was murdered by his fake brother, leaving me free to become a GI bride after my GI and his buddies had rescued me from being murdered in that dark alley because I had learned too much.

Somewhere along the way, my subconscious must have registered that Lazlo Tronnix bore a close resemblance to the villain in that film.

Not that that meant a thing. Not one single thing, I told myself firmly. You couldn't condemn a man on the off-chance that, in duplicating a certain set of features, Life could be imitating Art—not that any of *Vengeance in Vienna* could have been called Art, even by the most rabid of old film buffs.

'Trixie!' Evangeline had that imperious—some might say snappish—note in her voice she gets when people aren't paying enough attention to her. 'Lazlo asked you a question.'

'Oh, sorry. I was miles away.' I might as well admit it; they had already noticed I wasn't here. 'What is it?'

'I have a box at the Opera—' he began.

Of course he had. There had been that highly-publicized affaire with that famous Italian diva. Rumour had it that he had purchased a box in every leading opera house in the world. Before the even better-publicized break-up, that is.

'Personally, I find opera boring, pretentious and doom-laden, with everyone dying at great length—'

Uh-huh. When it's over, it's over.

'However, as an example of conspicuous consumption, a box at the opera is a proper investment. It is also excellent for corporate entertaining. Many business contacts appreciate the so-called glamour of being seen in such surroundings. Especially, their wives do. A box at the opera is really a satisfactory expenditure.'

Put that way, it was also tax-deductible. There's always

the vexed problem of what to do with leftover souvenirs once the romance has ended. The woman can always send back the jewellery if she's so inclined—not many of them are. The man accumulates different mementoes, sometimes more awkward ones. A box at the opera can't be wrapped up and sent back so easily.

I found myself starting to hum, '*These foolish things remind me of you . . .*' and stopped abruptly. I don't think Lazlo caught it.

'Trixie!' Evangeline had. Her voice was poisonously sweet and pulsated with warning.

'Forgive me, I digress too much.' Lazlo realized he was losing his audience. 'What I mean to say is: would you be so kind as to honour me with your presence in my box on Saturday evening of next week? I believe they are performing *Norma*, one of the few of these faragoes to have a happy ending.'

'Sounds good to me.' Not all that good, actually, but my conscience was still a bit sensitive because of what I had been thinking about him. He couldn't help looking like the villain in a wartime film. Besides, that villain had been a charming home-loving man and devoted husband and father in real life.

'Excellent.' He relaxed. 'Evangeline also has agreed and I shall invite some business acquaintances and their wives to complete the party. We will dine in Covent Garden before or after the performance, as you prefer.'

'Fine.' So it was to be another Display on the Town night. Somehow I hadn't doubted it. Lazlo was determined to hammer home the fact that he was very healthy and highly solvent.

The telephone and the doorbell rang simultaneously.

'Such a busy day,' Evangeline murmured, obviously deciding the telephone was the more promising of the two. She left the door to me, since all it had entailed so far was manual labour heaving bouquets and potted plants around. I heard her cooing into the telephone as I opened the door.

'Oh, it's you, Jasper.' I hoped I didn't sound disappointed. Actually, I was relieved that it wasn't more flowers. The place was beginning to resemble a florist's shop.

'Trixie, congratulations! I think you made the front page of every newspaper in Town.' Jasper beamed warmly, even as he craned over my shoulder to look behind me. 'Great publicity. Absolutely great.'

Did he think some of it was going to rub off on him? The newspapers hadn't given our address. Of course, Jasper could take care of that—as he handed round the brochures for the unsold flats.

'Come in.' If I was less than enthusiastic, he didn't notice. He was moving forward anyway, crowding me out of his way, still looking beyond me. I didn't think it was Evangeline he was so anxious to see—and it wasn't.

'Lazlo, I've been trying to reach you. I wondered if you were here.'

'Like a bee to a honeypot. I find my new neighbours irresistible.' Lazlo's look suggested that he was able to resist Jasper quite easily. 'We are making future plans.' The words were unexceptional, but something in the intonation implied that Jasper's future might be in doubt.

'Umm, good.' Jasper's self-confidence seemed to nosedive. He regarded Lazlo anxiously, evidently having second thoughts about whatever he had wanted to see him about.

'Oh, really!' Evangeline's voice rose sharply and I realized she had lost the cooing note several sentences ago. I could tell that she was regretting her choice of the telephone rather than the door. 'Well, let me assure you, Job, that we did not go out on the Town solely to get publicity for your new film! Such a thought never crossed our minds.'

'In fact, we're trying to forget,' I murmured.

'*No*, Job!' Evangeline's voice choked with outrage. 'We will *not* come back and do a dancing-on-the-tables sequence to be cut into the film! *NO*, not even if you arrange for it to be shot in a London studio. We'd see you in hell first! In fact, I'd prefer to see you in hell anyway!'

'Ah . . .' Lazlo sighed enviously. 'How I could do with her on my Board of Directors.'

Evangeline slammed down the phone and turned to me, breathing hard. 'The *nerve* of that man! The unmitigated gall!'

'I suppose you can't blame him for trying.' After all, since we'd made the film to begin with, he must think we were a couple of patsies.

'I'd blame him for anything!' Evangeline was unforgiving. She looked around, as if for something to throw.

'Never mind.' I moved in front of the nearest portable potted plant. 'It's over now and we don't have to see him again. Ever.'

'And *that* will be too soon!' She subsided on to a chair, still brooding.

'Forget him!' Lazlo seconded me vehemently. 'He is of the past. *We* have the future to consider!'

Uh-oh! I exchanged a swift apprehensive glance with Evangeline. Surely he wasn't . . . ?

'I have reserved a table at *The Gliding Gourmet* for Sunday luncheon. You will be my guests and we will plan further action.' He beamed at Evangeline guilelessly. 'I will have you on my Board of Directors yet.'

He was. We'd met these types before. Give them an inch and they thought they could take over your life. The forest was full of them and celebrities who hadn't learned how to avoid them didn't last long.

'Actually,' Evangeline said distantly, 'we already have a reservation for *The Gliding Gourmet*. And we will be bringing our own guests.'

'Forgive me.' He could take a snub, give him that. And he knew when he was out of line. 'I am presumptuous. Naturally, you will have plans of your own. We have only just met.'

'Quite.' Evangeline was still distant.

Jasper had begun twitching, as though afraid any slight shown to Lazlo might rebound on him. Especially if Lazlo discovered he was one of the guests. But . . . who was the other? Evangeline hadn't told me.

'Er . . .' Jasper dithered. 'Perhaps we should be going . . .'

Before one of us let drop that he was to be our guest. By Sunday, the atmosphere would have settled down and Lazlo would be in a better mood to make the discovery.

'You said,' Jasper reminded him, 'you wanted to . . . speak to me.'

'I do.' Lazlo's eyes narrowed unpleasantly. Yes, Jasper was in for an uncomfortable interlude, all right. I thought briefly of trying to do something to lighten the situation, like suggesting Lazlo might join us for drinks before or after lunch. Very briefly. That would have let *me* in for a nasty interlude with Evangeline after they had left. Too bad, but Jasper was on his own.

'My compliments, ladies.' Lazlo gave a stiff bow. 'I trust you will excuse an abrupt departure. When next we meet, perhaps you will permit me to arrange another social occasion. At suitable notice, of course.'

'That would be lovely.' I found myself gushing as I trailed them to the door. 'And thank you so much for the exquisite pins. You really shouldn't have,' I added politely, if unconvincingly.

'It was my pleasure,' he said, just as unconvincingly.

I think I managed to get the door closed behind them in time to keep him from hearing Evangeline's '*Huummmmph!*'

'All right,' I said, facing her. 'I give up. Who's our other guest for Sunday?'

'Oh well,' she bridled, delighted that I'd had to ask. 'I thought I'd invite that charming Detective-Superintendent Hay-Hee.'

'You wouldn't—' I broke off. Yes, she would. She'd dare anything. I settled for a more certain statement:

'He'd never come.'

'You think not?' She quirked one eyebrow and gave me a maddeningly superior smile. 'Just wait and see.'

CHAPTER 8

After the chill along the river, *The Gliding Gourmet* was comparatively cosy. There was still a certain amount of chill emanating from Detective-Superintendent Heyhoe, but he was gradually warming up under the combined influence of Evangeline's concentrated charm and the magnum of champagne she had provided from our offerings.

Personally, I thought she was overdoing the charm, but Heyhoe seemed to be going for it hook, line and almost sinker. Only the occasional sideways shift of his eyes betrayed that he had not relinquished all his distrust. Why was she being so nice to him? What did she want?

I had wondered that myself, before remembering that Jasper had been inquiring after our policeman friends, clearly with a view to an informal meeting. Now that Evangeline had provided it, he seemed to be in no hurry to take advantage of it. Or perhaps he considered this the initial social encounter and would set up his own appointment with Heyhoe for a private conversation at another time. When we weren't around to hear what he had to say . . . or confess.

'Let me top you up.' Jasper poured champagne lavishly into Heyhoe's glass, taking full advantage of Evangeline's request that he 'do the honours'.

'Ah, thank you.' Heyhoe relaxed a millimetre more. He almost smiled. For the first time since he had walked into our penthouse flourishing a bouquet of modest spring blossoms: freesias, daffodils, irises and mimosa—only to stop short and look around for a place to hide what now looked like a paltry offering as he saw the opulent displays turning our drawing-room into a version of a florist's shop, a very expensive florist's shop.

We had cooed and exclaimed over his bouquet, of course, but he knew that he'd been hopelessly outclassed. And there is nothing that upsets an Englishman more.

It had taken all this time to coax him into a moderately good humour. And there were moments when I wondered why Evangeline was bothering. It was most unlike her.

The Gliding Gourmet was warming up, too, and beginning to take on a party-like air. Enormous platters of antipasto and wicker baskets heaped with garlic bread had been placed on each table and everyone had brought their own bottles of wine. The place was almost full and, judging from the platters of antipasto waiting on the few empty tables, there were still more customers expected.

I looked around and spotted Hamish at an adjoining table with three young men I hadn't seen before; they must be the other members of The Chummery.

He winked and raised his glass to me, saying something to the others as he did so. They all turned and raised their glasses. I winked back and raised my own glass. It was obviously going to be convivial gathering.

As I let my gaze rove around the dining salon, I couldn't help noticing more than one of the youngsters palming slices of salami and rolls and slipping them into pockets and handbags. Tomorrow's breakfast, no doubt. Well, I'd done the same myself when times were tough and the opportunity offered. It happens to the best of us.

Most of the diners appeared to be from our warehouse. Of course, there weren't many other inhabited buildings in the vicinity. It was practically a family occasion—unless the empty tables were going to be occupied by strangers.

I brought my attention back to our own table, where Evangeline was telling Heyhoe how well Julian was doing with his scriptwriting. Heyhoe did not look enchanted to hear it. Jasper splashed more champagne into our glasses and Evangeline gave him an approving smile. Delicious aromas were wafting out from the galley. The noise level had risen by several decibels and laughter began breaking out among the diners. The cares of the week were being forgotten.

Nigel, looking more relaxed than I had yet seen him, was at the table facing me, with Roz and two other girls I didn't recognize. More neighbours, I had no doubt.

I let my gaze drift past Evangeline to look across the river to the opposite shore. The river seemed very high, small waves danced on the surface and there was a barely noticeable slap-slap-slap against the hull of the boat. I relaxed into the faint sway; I had almost forgotten how pleasant it was to be on the water. It was a long time since I had taken a sea voyage; it seemed pointless just to go cruising and there weren't all that many ships crossing the oceans any more. Still, it would be very pleasant to—

The sudden hiss of a sharply-indrawn breath snapped me out of my reverie. I realized that I had heard it because the room had abruptly gone silent. All eyes were turned towards the entrance, with varying degrees of hostility.

Lazlo Tronnix stood there beaming. Mariah stood beside him, his guest, a tentative placatory smile on her lips. She knew who the hostility was aimed at.

She seemed like such a pleasant, harmless young woman.

I looked incredulously at the naked faces in that split-second before they adjusted their masks again. The expressions showed not only hostility, but horror, loathing and, yes, fear.

Lazlo had appeared at their feast with the skeleton on his arm all right. Had he done it deliberately?

Behind him hovered a couple of Suits, filled with bland anonymous young men who could only be employees. Mid-management-aiming-for-senior, I'd say, but the deference-bordering-on-fawning was unmistakable. They didn't notice anything about the atmosphere as they stepped into it. I suspected that that alone was going to disqualify them from rising to the senior posts they coveted. Lazlo was not one to suffer fools gladly—or at all. I was amazed that they had lasted this far.

They didn't like Mariah, either. She stumbled on the low step down into the salon and it was Lazlo who caught her arm. The other two stood motionless, their faces deadpan, but with a flicker of malice in their eyes: they wanted her to fall.

She was certainly the most unpopular woman I had ever seen. Outside the profession, that is.

Even Sophie faltered momentarily as she emerged from the gallery and went forward to meet Lazlo and lead him to his table. It was right behind us, Evangeline and I had our backs to it. I couldn't ask Jasper or Heyhoe to change seats with me. Too bad.

Conversations began again, more subdued. The burgeoning hilarity had slipped away; things weren't so funny now.

Mariah gazed longingly at Jasper as they passed and I could see from his expression that she had seated herself facing him. He sent a weak smile in her direction, then concentrated all his attention on our antipasto, meticulously choosing one black olive as though there were a difference between it and all the others in the heap. He transferred it to his mouth, closed his eyes and savoured it: a true connoisseur—and much too absorbed to catch anyone's eye.

'Who's that?' Detective-Superintendent Heyhoe had gone on to full alert, the tip of his nose twitched suspiciously and there was a look in his eyes suggesting that he was mentally flipping through a file of mugshots.

'Who?' Evangeline blinked and looked around vaguely, but she wasn't kidding me. She, too, was consumed with curiosity.

'Those people who just came in.' Heyhoe spoke softly, biting off each word; Evangeline wasn't kidding him any, either. 'They look vaguely familiar. At least,' he qualified, 'the big man does.'

'Lazlo Tronnix,' I said quickly, before Evangeline could make a production out of it and get him even more suspicious. 'He's some sort of financier/inventor/manufacturer. He has his own conglomerate: Multitronics International.'

'Mmmmm . . . and the woman?'

'Mariah Lacey. She's, er . . . she's . . .' I realized I had no idea what she was.

'His mistress?' Heyhoe mistook my hesitation for discretion.

'Certainly not!' Jasper yelped indignantly. 'She doesn't even know him.'

'Mmmm?' Heyhoe selected an olive of his own. 'They seem to be getting along very well . . . for strangers.' He looked across at the other table and, in a superb piece of theatre—I didn't know he had it in him—abruptly raised both eyebrows and bulged out his eyes. '*Very* well, indeed.'

Wouldn't you just know that both Evangeline and I would be sitting with our backs to that table? I nearly dislocated something vital trying to crane my neck to look casually over my shoulder. Evangeline was doing the same. Jasper crunched down on a length of celery with a violence that threatened to break a tooth.

All that came into my line of vision was the well-tailored back of one of the Suits. It looked rigid, unyielding and disapproving—no better than one would have expected from a Suit.

Evangeline's exasperated snort told me that she hadn't had any better luck, but something pretty fascinating must have been happening back there because Jasper was turning an interesting shade of mauve and grinding his teeth; the fact that he now had a piece of salami between them was only incidental.

'What *does* she do?' Heyhoe was not going to let the subject drop. He had unerringly pinpointed her as the cause of the ripple of unease that had disrupted the party atmosphere.

'Nothing,' Jasper said savagely. 'At least, nothing you'd be interested in. Her work is perfectly legal.'

'What makes you think I'm only interested in the illegal? Anyway, I'm off duty now and out of my manor. Anything going on here would have nothing to do with me.' Perhaps, if his smile had been less sharklike, we might have believed him. Perhaps.

Jasper bit off a huge chunk of garlic bread and chewed stubbornly. He couldn't talk with his mouth full, could he?

Evangeline and I exchanged despairing glances. This was not going to be one of our social successes. If Jasper had ever had anything he wanted to discuss with Heyhoe, it was now obvious that he had abandoned the idea. He wouldn't have given Heyhoe the right time of day, never mind ask advice of him.

Sophie and Frederick conducted an organized swoop on the tables, clearing away the empty antipasto platters preparatory to bringing in the entrée. A rustle of anticipation stirred the air.

There was the sudden roar of a motorboat speeding past on the far side of the river and a murmur of indignation arose.

'He's going much too fast,' Jasper said. 'Brace yourselves. It's going to be rough when the wash hits us.'

'Isn't it against the law to speed like that on the river?' I was already gripping the edge of the table firmly as I watched a low wall of water eddy towards us.

'That's for the River Police to deal with!' Heyhoe seemed to take my question as an implied criticism. He eyed the approaching tidal wave uneasily.

'It's definitely against the unwritten law of the river,' Jasper said. 'I don't know whether there's an actual law against it, but it's dangerous and discourteous to the other boats on the river. Boats are supposed to cut their speed when they're passing other boats and moored craft.'

There were screams and shouts from the unwary diners at other tables as the first wave hit us, hurling us against the dock. There was also an ominous crash from the galley.

Then came a series of judders and jars as we were battered against the dock by the succession of diminishing waves of the wash. When the last ripple died away, I sat there still clutching the table and trying to convince myself that you couldn't get seasick while you were still tied up to the dock. Detective-Superintendent Heyhoe had gone a little green around the gills himself, I was cheered to notice.

'Some people—' Evangeline helped herself to another chunk of garlic bread and bit into it with gusto—'some people have no consideration for others. They ought to be locked up!'

'There's nothing I can do about it.' Again, Heyhoe sensed criticism; for an instant, his glance left no doubt about who he would like to lock up. 'And I'm sure the

River Police have more to worry about than a few careless boaters.'

'I hope that crash in the kitchen wasn't something important.' Evangeline decided to change the subject. 'I'm hungry.'

'Just a stack of empty platters,' Frederick said bravely, if unconvincingly, stalking down the aisle between the tables and dealing out small dishes of finely-chopped garlic and chilli peppers.

They were obviously intended for those who preferred their dishes highly-spiced, but I decided they'd also act as germ-killers if any of the menu had had to be scraped up off the floor before serving. ('Bring in the *other* turkey,' as the quick-witted hostess said to the maid who dropped the turkey on the floor in front of the dinner-party.)

The thought seemed not to have occurred to anyone else. The hum of enthusiasm rose as Sophie appeared, bearing steaming bowls of something fragrant but unidentifiable— at least by me.

The others had no trouble recognizing it. Someone raised a cheer and someone else started a ragged chorus of '*For they are jolly good fellows* . . .' It was obviously a great favourite.

Whatever it was—some sort of supersophisticated pasta—it was delicious. Second helpings were freely offered and almost everyone accepted, although Jasper sounded a warning:

'Save a bit of room for the dessert. Sophie is famous for—'

A piercing scream slashed through the room. One of the young women at Roz's table leaped to her feet, her chair clattering as it struck the floor, and pressed herself against the window, still screaming. The others crowded around her at the window, trying to see what had set her off. They began screaming, too.

'Oh, for heaven's sake!' Evangeline pushed back her

chair and leaned against our window. I was right behind her.

In the moment before I saw it, I became aware of a strange irregular thumping against the hull of our craft. Not the slap-slap of the waves we had heard before, but a softer, more muted sound, almost as though someone were knocking to come in.

There was another soft thump and the body rolled away from the boat and lay atop a wave, seeming to brace itself for a fresh assault. It was female, but the features seemed to have blurred and the skin was a pale, pale blue. I looked away quickly. She must have been in the water a long time.

'I might have known it,' Heyhoe muttered. His accusing glare told Evangeline she had arranged this specially for him. As an afterthought, he swivelled to include me in it. We were both tarred with the same brush and he should have known better than to expect anything good of us.

The boat tilted sharply as everyone rushed to our side to look out on the river. There was another crash from the galley.

'Even though this isn't your territory,' Evangeline prodded Heyhoe, 'you *are* a policeman. Shouldn't you *do* something?'

For a split-second something nasty flashed in his eyes and I thought he was going to hit her. Frankly, I'd have had every sympathy. But that rigid control prevailed and he merely opened his mouth for a verbal answer. Before he could do so, another shrill scream reverberated through the saloon as the body rolled closer to the boat again.

'I think—' The screamer pushed herself away from the window, leaving room for someone else to take her place. Her eyes sought Nigel, who was just rising from his chair. 'Oh, Nigel—I think it's Sandra!'

The others fell back from that window, leaving an aisle for Nigel to walk slowly, his face blank with incredulity.

'It can't be,' he said. 'No. No, she ran out on me, that's all. Things . . . just overwhelmed her. Temporarily. She'll be back. You'll see . . .'

He was at the window now, trying not to look out. 'I know the way her mind works,' he explained earnestly to the others. 'She just needed a rest. To get away for a while. I'm expecting her back any min—'

He was interrupted by another soft thud against the hull. Involuntarily, he glanced out the window.

'Oh God!' He turned green and pitched forward, cracking his head against the glass and sliding to the floor.

'I told you it was Sandra,' the screamer said.

CHAPTER 9

'Sandra?' Sophie had come out of the galley in response to the screaming. Now she started forward, but Frederick caught her from behind, holding on tightly.

'That's it! Don't let her near the window, for God's sake!' Roz's voice was unsteady.

'Let me go!' Sophie fought to free herself. 'She's my sister! I have the right to see—'

'No, honestly.' Jasper went to help Frederick. 'You don't want to see. Believe me, you don't want to.'

Evangeline had left the table, too, but moved in the opposite direction. I watched unbelievingly as she knelt beside Nigel and began going through his pockets.

Detective-Superintendent Heyhoe stared at her with gloomy anticipation. Again, it seemed to be no more than he expected—and this time he had her dead to rights.

I tried to convince myself that he probably couldn't arrest her unless she actually transferred Nigel's wallet into her own handbag. Probably.

Sophie burst into tears as Frederick forced her down into a chair. Jasper offered her a glass of champagne. She pushed it away impatiently.

There was another soft thud against the hull . . . farther along. The body was drifting with the tide . . . and the tide has turned.

'Shouldn't we *do* something?' one of the men from The Chummery asked uneasily. 'Try to get her ashore? Before she's carried out to sea?'

'Sandra!' Sophie lurched to her feet, swayed for a moment, then slipped to the floor before Frederick or Jasper could catch her.

'Here we are!' Evangeline found what she was looking for. She pulled the cellphone from Nigel's pocket and handed it to Detective-Superintendent Heyhoe.

'You'd better use this to ring the River Police,' she said. 'They'll want to collect that body before they lose it.'

'I didn't know Sophie and Sandra were sisters,' Evangeline complained.

'There was no reason why you should.' Jasper was not in a good mood, either. 'You never knew Sandra at all.'

We were back in our penthouse. Detective-Superintendent Heyhoe had gone off with the River Police after bidding us an abrupt and glacial farewell. Something told us not to hold our breaths waiting for the thank-you note for a memorable afternoon.

'As a matter of fact,' Jasper decided to explain, 'that's why Sophie and Frederick are here. They ran a snack bar and restaurant down on the South Coast, but when Sandra moved in here with Nigel, she was so enthusiastic about the opportunities Docklands offered that she persuaded Sophie and Frederick to move. They'd always wanted to shift upmarket and the set-up seemed ideal. Of course,' he added gloomily, 'that was just before the bottom started to fall out of everything.'

Including Jasper's own life and plans, I suspected. He sank into a brooding silence, staring out at the long shimmering vista of the river.

It didn't look so romantic to me right now—not when I knew the sort of things that were dragged out of it.

'At least—' I tried to think of something positive. 'At least, Nigel knows now that she didn't run out on him. There was some kind of accident—'

'Was there?' Evangeline asked caustically. 'Or did he get rid of her himself? For whatever reasons of his own?'

'You can't think that!' Jasper blanched. 'You saw poor Nigel. He was devastated.'

'That might have been because she floated to the surface, jarred loose from whatever had been holding her down by all the wash from that speedboat. By this time, Nigel would have thought that the body had been carried out to sea. And he was safe.'

'No!' Jasper shook his head. 'I won't listen to you. You turn everything into a second-rate melodrama. Life isn't like that. It isn't a cheap movie.'

Evangeline's eyes narrowed. If looks could kill, Jasper would have been bobbing his way down towards the Thames Barrier himself.

'Really, Evangeline—' I began.

'Did you see the back of her head when they pulled her out?' Evangeline demanded.

We both shook our heads. I was pretty certain that Jasper, like me, had closed his eyes as the body was heaved on to the shore.

'It wasn't there,' Evangeline said graphically. 'You can't tell me a wound like that could have been caused by merely hitting her head against something as she fell into the river. Not even the fish could have caused such damage.'

We lost Jasper at that point. He went a pale pistachio and dived for the bathroom.

I managed to hold my ground, but it wasn't easy. I felt myself swaying. The only defence was a counter-attack.

'Now look what you've done! Poor Jasper—'

'Poor Jasper. Poor Nigel,' Evangeline jeered. 'What about poor Sandra? And poor Sophie? It's the ones who are left behind who have the worst burden to bear.'

She'd silenced me. There was no argument on that one.

'Anyway—' I approached it from another angle—'why should Nigel want to kill Sandra?'

'He wouldn't.' Jasper reappeared, pale but determined. 'He needed her. Desperately. They were financially interdependent.'

'That sounds like a true love match,' Evangeline said.

'It was,' Jasper insisted. 'Nigel was blown to pieces when she disappeared. He couldn't believe it. He was sure she was coming back to him when she'd cooled off.'

'And what did she have to cool off from?' Evangeline pounced.

'Oh, they had their little arguments,' Jasper said evasively. 'Who doesn't?'

'About what?' Evangeline was not going to let him off that easily.

'Oh, well, money, of course.' Jasper wriggled his shoulders uncomfortably. 'What else, these days?'

'Money, of course.' Evangeline nodded. 'An eternally sensitive subject. Especially when you haven't enough of it.'

'Not many people have.' Jasper winced, although the dart had not been aimed at him particularly. 'Not around here. Not anywhere, these days.'

'But especially not around here.'

'You know how it is. People bought their flats at the height of the boom. I won't say they paid too much for them—' (Well, he wouldn't, would he? He was the one they paid.)

'But the market didn't stand up the way everyone thought it would. The crash came. People lost their jobs or had to take pay cuts. Their financial situations became unmanageable. They all had other debts, too: credit cards, fancy cars, a place in the country. The whole flaming lot!' His voice turned bitter.

'We were being urged on all sides to "gear up". We were told we weren't maximizing our potential unless we were carrying as much debt as we could "service"—and maybe more. Because property values were just going to go up and up. And so were salaries. And we couldn't lose . . .'

'Until you found out that you could.' Evangeline sighed.

We'd seen it all happening before, but on a more personal scale, usually. Whole generations hadn't been thrown into bankruptcy since the Crash of 1929 and the ensuing Depression.

I caught myself humming, '*Brother, Can You Spare a Dime?*' and stopped abruptly. Luckily, Jasper hadn't noticed.

'I suppose,' Jasper went on thoughtfully, 'it's not too surprising that Sandra should kill herself. There were so many pressures on her. She was paying all the bills on the flat and the mortgage since Nigel lost his job. She'd loaned a lot of money to Sophie and Frederick, too, with no immediate prospects of getting it back—'

'I thought Lazlo was backing Sophie and Frederick,' I said.

'He is now. But, in the beginning, it was Sandra who took on the financing for buying the boat, rebuilding it as a restaurant and equipping it. Tronnix has just stepped in lately, now that they're moving ashore and into the building.'

'Which is another considerable expense,' Evangeline murmured. 'They're very lucky to have his help.'

'Right,' Jasper said. 'Except—that was a large part of

the trouble. Nigel had begun nagging Sandra to get her money back from Sophie out of the money Tronnix was lending her.'

Evangeline snorted and I felt a nasty noise trying to escape my own lips. Our opinion of Nigel wasn't improving, the more we learned about him. From trying to start a run on Lazlo's shares to badgering his girlfriend about her own money while he was living off her, Nigel was beginning to sound like some of the sleazier Hollywood hangers-on we had met.

'They were having quite a few fights over it,' Jasper admitted unsurprisingly. 'I think Sandra was getting pretty fed up. Old Nigel has a tendency to bore on and on until he gets his own way. I wouldn't have blamed her a bit if she'd decided to decamp. But this—' He broke off and shuddered.

'I wouldn't jump to conclusions, if I were you,' Evangeline said. 'She doesn't sound suicidal to me. And you didn't see the back of her head when they pulled her out of the water!'

'No.' He shuddered again. 'No. I—I couldn't look.'

'It could have been an accident,' I said firmly. 'We've had a lot of cold weather and icy rain. She might have slipped and hit her head—'

'The *back* of her head?' Evangeline raised a disbelieving eyebrow. 'A dent *that* deep? She was probably dead before she hit the water. It couldn't have happened naturally. It looked as though something—someone—hit her with enormous force.'

'Don't *say* such things!' Jasper was in a bad way. Of course, he had known the girl. It was all very well for Evangeline to theorize; when you'd never known the victim, you could be dispassionate about her fate. Jasper would have memories of her alive and laughing.

So would Sophie. Especially Sophie. Poor Sophie.

'How is Sophie?' I asked.

'Under sedation.' Jasper seemed surprised that I didn't
know. 'Naturally. There were just the two of them, parents
dead. They were very close. Frederick is going to have his
hands full over the next few weeks.'

'Frederick . . .' Evangeline pursed her lips thoughtfully.
'Jealous of his sister-in-law, was he? Maybe he thought
Sophie paid too much attention to Sandra and not enough
to him? Or was he afraid that Sandra might decide, after
all, that she wanted her money back? Now, I suppose
Sophie will inherit everything and they won't have to worry
about repaying the loan.'

'My God!' Jasper stared at her, aghast. 'You—you don't
know what you're saying. It's just a game to you. Another
scenario to play with. You—you're not even human!' He
turned and ran for the door, one hand over his mouth, as
though he was afraid he might say something worse. Or
perhaps he was going to be sick again.

The door slammed behind him.

'He's right, you know,' I pointed out. 'This isn't just
another episode of *The Happy Couple*. These people are real.
They hurt, they bleed—'

'There wouldn't have been much blood, I think. Not even
before the water leached it all away. The blow imploded the
skull inwards, there was just the deep dent on the surface.'

I headed for the brandy decanter. It must have been all
those *Happy Couple* mysteries she had starred in; staring at
bodies didn't bother her a bit. Down deep, she probably
thought it was all make-up. I hadn't been able to look close;
I knew the difference.

'Pour one for me,' Evangeline commanded. ' "Unt don't
be stingy" ,' she added in a good imitation of Garbo's accent
in *Anna Christie*.

But it wasn't quite a joke, I realized as I turned to her
with the drink. She had gone very white and she snatched

at the glass thankfully and took a large gulp. After a long moment, her colour began to return.

'You shouldn't have looked so closely at that body,' I said. None of us needed that much reminder of our mortality.

'It was my only chance,' Evangeline defended. 'I knew that, once the police had taken it away, we'd never see it again.'

'I should hope not!' The thought was so disturbing, I finished my brandy more quickly than I had intended. 'It's nothing to do with us. Nothing!' I emphasized firmly.

'You may be right.' Evangeline sounded unconvinced. 'But if something is going on in this building—'

'Then it's time we got out of it. Even if we do have to forfeit the rent we've already paid. It will be worth it.'

'Pour us another drink and stop being ridiculous.'

I complied with the first request but, so far as she was concerned, ignored the second.

'I'm being sensible, not ridiculous—and you know it.'

Evangeline accepted her recharged snifter and sauntered over to the windows framing the panorama of the river, humming maddeningly.

'*Evangeline* . . .' I snarled.

'We're really lucky to be living here, Trixie. Lots of people would envy us. Look at the view—' She gestured to the river below. 'The Thames . . . liquid history . . . flowing endlessly . . . from time immemorial . . . bearing conqueror and defeated . . .'

'Evangeline . . .'

'The river used to be alive with traffic. Ships from all over the world sailed into the Pool of London, bringing cargo and passengers. "*From distant Ophir* . . ." Oh—' She hammed it up, one hand to her throat with her best soulful look. 'Can't you appreciate the romance of the river?'

'It didn't look very romantic when they dragged that body out of it.'

'All part of its history, a part we happened to witness. You can't blame the river for what people do to it.'

'I've got nothing against the river,' I said. 'I'd just like to live farther along it. Closer to civilization. Anywhere between Blackfriars Bridge and Chelsea Bridge would suit me just fine.'

'*Pah!*' But there was a wistful look in her own eye as she turned away from the window. 'Well, perhaps we'll see about it,' she conceded. '*After* we've come to the end of our rental term here.'

CHAPTER 10

There are some days when you feel you've just had enough. Too much, in fact. Especially where Evangeline was concerned.

It was time to spend a day apart, perhaps two or three days. We'd both feel better for it. But the weather was still vile and all our friends were still out of town. There was also the delicate problem of broaching the subject to Evangeline. Fortunately, she was way ahead of me.

'I have some errands I can't put off any longer.' Evangeline came into the drawing-room wearing her coat and pulling on her gloves. 'Would you like to share a taxi to the West End?'

'I don't think so, thanks.' I tried to keep the relief out of my voice. An afternoon to myself—and I didn't have to go out for it.

'I should think you'd be glad to escape for a while,' she said. 'You complain enough about the place. Even I've got cabin fever, cooped up here.' She made it sound like the tiny cabin in which Charlie Chaplin was snowbound with the heavy in *The Gold Rush*.

The telephone rang; she pounced on it and listened intently before replacing it.

'The taxi is waiting downstairs. Sure you won't change your mind?'

'I'll wait till the weather improves.'

'You'll be rattling around here alone.' She gave me a sharp suspicious look as she went out of the door. 'I don't know what you'll find to do with yourself all day.'

'I'll think of something.' I waved as the door closed behind her.

For the first hour, I just relaxed and enjoyed the space and silence. A couple of hours later, I began to grow a mite restless. I'd done my workout, sneered at the afternoon television, flipped through the magazines again—and it was still raining. I let myself decide to do what I had been intending to do all along: I would call on some of the neighbours.

I'd start with those I could be certain I'd find at home in the afternoon: a condolence call was due, anyway. I roamed out into the kitchen, trying to think of something suitable to bring along as an offering and an excuse. Would it be faintly insulting to give store-bought baked goods to a professional cook? If only Martha were here, she could whip up a batch of her apple-spice cookies in no time and I could deliver them still warm from the oven; that would be more like it. But Martha was on the other side of the ocean and I had neither the time nor the inclination to mess around in that spaceship of a kitchen, trying to subdue the menacing oven.

I settled on the last unopened bottle of brandy. That would be quite suitable and, if they didn't like it, they could always dump it in the puddings.

'Oh . . .' Frederick opened the door and seemed

surprised, but not displeased to see me. 'Hello, Trixie.'

'I just dropped by to say how sorry I am and to see how Sophie is doing.' I thrust the bottle of brandy at him. 'This isn't exactly a home-baked pie, but I hope it will come in handy.'

'Oh, thanks.' Frederick took it and glanced at the label appreciatively. 'It certainly will. We could have done with this last night.'

There would be plenty of difficult nights to come, but I didn't need to tell him that; he knew it himself.

'Come in.' He stepped back from the doorway. 'I'll get Sophie. She's just lying down.'

'I wouldn't want to disturb her.' I stepped into the room quickly before he could take me at my word.

'No, no,' he assured me. 'Best thing for her, a little company. Especially someone who has nothing to do with this whole nightmare. I mean—' He shrugged and turned away, leaving me alone in the long empty room that would eventually become a restaurant . . . or would it, now?

At least, I thought I was alone, until I heard a throat cleared behind me. I turned to find Nigel standing there. For a moment, my courage failed me. Whatever one thought of him, Nigel had been Sandra's lover. I wasn't sure I could cope with both the seriously bereaved at the same time. I'd had Nigel marked down for a separate visit.

'Hello.' He stood there staring at me plaintively.

'Nigel, I'm so very sorry. How *are* you?'

'Thanks.' He nodded glumly, then burst out: 'You know, I'd rather she left me! Even if she wasn't coming back. Anything rather than this!'

'Yes, dear, I know.' Oh, heavens, it was going to be worse than I'd thought. How did I get into these things? He was blinking heavily. He wasn't going to cry, was he?

How much better any of my old co-stars would have handled the scene, in the best stiff-upper-lip English tradition. A sardonic remark, a tilt of the eyebrow, and only a sudden flash of pain in the eyes and a swift shadow passing across the face to betray the deep emotion. But whatever Nigel had that was stiff, it was not his upper lip.

'You never knew her,' he quavered.

'No, but having met Sophie—'

'She was nothing like Sophie! *She* had a heart!' He took a deep breath and shook his head as though to clear it. 'Too much of a heart. Everyone took advantage of her.'

'You ought to know.' A cold voice spoke from across the room. 'You were leading the pack.'

'Funny, I could have sworn *you* were ahead of me!' Nigel whirled to face the challenge.

'Why is he still here?' Sophie turned to her husband. 'I told him to leave.'

'Oh, now, you can't treat poor Nigel like that,' Frederick said uncomfortably. 'He's practically your brother-in-law.'

'Oh no, he isn't!' Sophie snapped. 'Get him out of here!'

'No, really,' Frederick said gently. 'We can't do that. You don't mean it. You're both upset, grieving.' It seemed that Frederick had a heart of his own. 'You should be supporting each other at a time like this, not fighting.'

'Supporting is the right word! Now that he's lost Sandra, he thinks we're going to be fools enough to support him!'

'I'd never dream of it,' Nigel snarled. 'You can't even support yourselves. Sandra was subsidizing you every inch of the way.'

'I picked a bad time to call,' I apologized to anyone who happened to be listening. 'Perhaps I'd better come back later.' I began edging towards the door.

'No!' Sophie's hand shot out and clamped a steel-like band around my arm. '*You're* not the one I want to leave!'

'Please stay, Trixie.' Less forcefully, Frederick seconded his wife's request. 'I think it would . . . be better.'

'Would you believe it?' Having recognized a new audience, Sophie appealed to me. 'This little . . . *twerp* . . . has had the nerve to come down here and *demand* repayment of the money *my* sister loaned to *me!* It's nothing to do with him at all.'

'Oh yes it is,' Nigel said. 'That money was joint property. I was her common law husband.'

'Common law isn't good enough,' Sophie sneered. 'It just means she retained enough sense not to actually marry you.'

'I really think I ought to be going.' I tried to tug away from that unrelenting grip. 'I'm expecting a telephone call . . .'

'Is that so?' Nigel was stung. 'She'd have married me in a minute if you hadn't always been there belittling me and telling her she could do a lot better.'

'Really, I—' But there was no escaping that iron grip. Why hadn't I gone to town with Evangeline?

'I suppose you asked her?' Sophie glared at him. 'Go ahead and tell me you ever asked her. *You* were the one who never wanted to commit yourself because you thought *you* could do better. She told me all about that little episode between you and the boss's daughter—when you *had* a boss. But that girl was no fool, either. And you needn't think you're fooling anyone with all your protestations now!'

The doorbell cut across the recriminations. Sophie was startled and her grip relaxed. I pulled myself free and retreated a safe distance while Frederick answered the door.

'Frederick, I hope I'm not intruding.' Roz stood there, clutching a Fortnum & Mason box.

'Roz, come in.' There was relief in Frederick's voice. With a larger audience, the hostilities would have to be suspended until a more private moment.

'I—I thought you might not feel like doing any cooking.' Roz offered him the Fortnum & Mason box. (Another one who didn't trust her own cooking enough to offer it to a professional chef.) 'It's a game pie.'

'Wonderful! Thank you.' Frederick accepted it with

enthusiasm. 'You're right. We haven't even thought about food . . . Well, Sophie hasn't and it seemed unfeeling to mention the subject.'

'Hello, Roz.' Sophie turned to greet her. 'How sweet of you to come.'

Nigel took the opportunity to slide closer to the door. It seemed he was now ready to leave. I wasn't too anxious to remain, either.

'Sit down.' The invitation seemed to be extended to everyone—even Nigel. Sophie waved her hand indicating a cluster of chairs by one of the windows overlooking the river. Frederick stood between us and the door, smiling encouragingly.

'I can't stay long,' Roz murmured, moving towards a chair. 'I just wanted to . . . to say how sorry . . .' She looked from Sophie to Nigel. 'Sandra was such a good friend.'

'Ah! Yes!' Nigel edged closer, asserting his right to a share of the condolences. 'Yes, yes, she was. Everyone loved her.'

Not everyone, if Evangeline's theory was correct. I wondered what failing Sandra might have had. Perhaps, like Sophie, she had more of a temper than was at first apparent; tempers often ran in families. She might have started a fight with the wrong person.

'We'll miss her terribly,' Roz said. Whatever Sandra's real temperament might have been, *de mortuis* was the order of the day here. I wasn't going to learn anything to her detriment.

'When . . .' Roz began, then hesitated, but there was no delicate way to phrase it. 'When is the funeral?'

Sophie gave a low moan and turned away. Frederick moved forward and put a hand on her shoulder.

'We don't know yet.' Nigel had lost colour, he shook his head disbelievingly. 'We can't make any plans until the police release the . . .' He couldn't say it.

'*I'll* make the plans!' Sophie came back to life, fighting. 'You have nothing to do with it.'

Roz glanced at me uneasily, the undercurrents now apparent to her. I gave a slight shrug, trying to convey that, really, I didn't know a thing about it. Roz looked wistfully towards the door. So did I.

'Some tea?' Sophie made an effort and smiled bravely.

'No. No, thank you,' I said quickly.

'We don't want to put you to any trouble.' Uh-oh, I could have told Roz that was the wrong thing to say.

'No trouble at all,' Frederick said. 'I'll see to it.' He started for the curtained-off area, but the doorbell rang again and he swerved to answer it.

My back was to the door, but I heard the murmur of a female voice—and I saw the way the others stiffened. I took a mental bet with myself. And won.

'Look who's here,' Frederick said in a strained voice, leading Mariah up to Sophie.

'I won't stay,' Mariah said defensively, perhaps noting that Roz was already struggling out of her chair and Nigel was backing towards the door. 'I just dropped in to offer my condolences.' She held a bouquet of flowers out to Sophie.

'Thank you.' With an obvious effort, Sophie stopped in mid-recoil and forced a smile. 'How very kind of you.'

'Sit down, Mariah,' Frederick said. 'You're always welcome here.' He emphasized it just a bit too much. 'You know that.'

'Yes, do,' Sophie said. 'Frederick was just going to make tea. You've arrived just in time.'

'Well, um . . .' Roz was on her feet. 'I told you I couldn't stay. Nice to see you, Mariah. We . . . we must get together sometime . . . lunch, or something.'

'Yes,' Mariah said flatly. 'That would be nice.' She wasn't fool enough to attempt to pin Roz down to a definite time.

'I'll be in touch later.' Nigel spoke over Sophie's head to Frederick. 'You'll let me know when . . . when you . . . you hear anything?'

'We'll keep you informed,' Frederick assured him.

'Goodbye, Sophie, Frederick, Mariah—' I latched myself firmly on to the departing guests and followed them out into the vast reception area. When Frederick closed the door behind us, the others slumped limply, as though invisible strings had been cut. They looked down towards the communal lounge, but seemed to dismiss the idea immediately; it was too near the point of danger. At any moment, the door might open and Mariah emerge.

'Look,' I said brightly. 'We didn't get our tea, so why don't you come upstairs and have it with me? Or something stronger,' I added—they looked as though they could use it. 'It must be getting on for Happy Hour.'

'Ah!' Nigel was the first to rally. 'What a good idea!' He led the way to the lifts.

'Oh—' Roz looked as though she had just heard the first faint bugle notes of the US Cavalry charging across the horizon to save the beleaguered wagon train, but still he hesitated. 'We wouldn't want to put you to any trouble.'

'What's so hard about pouring something into a glass? Besides,' I added, suspecting I knew the reason for her hesitation, 'Evangeline has gone out for the day. I'd be quite pleased to have some company.'

'Oh yes, then.' Her face cleared; she did not have to decide whether she was more afraid of Evangeline than of Mariah catching up with her. She could safely hide out with me until that danger was past. Evangeline, I could understand. But Mariah . . . ?

'Ah!' Nigel threw himself down on the sofa and looked around expansively. 'Very nice. Old Jasper did a good job with this place. Lots of . . . ah . . . space.'

'Lots,' Roz agreed, looking into the distance for some more furniture. She obviously decided the chairs were too far away and perched on the sofa beside Nigel.

'That's right.' A sudden surge of loyalty to Jasper prevented me from agreeing with them about the sparseness of the furnishings. 'Evangeline and I like plenty of space of our own.'

'Quite,' Nigel said and Roz nodded agreement. If she had to share with Evangeline, she'd have wanted a lot of space too.

I did the hostess bit and got them comfortably settled with their drinks and nibbles before moving in for the kill.

'Tell me—' There was no subtle way to lead up to this. 'What's wrong with Mariah? She seems like a perfectly nice ordinary girl—and yet everyone avoids her like the plague.'

'Ah! You think so, do you?' Nigel looked at his drink unhappily, obviously regretting there was so much of it left. He then looked at Roz, clearly tossing the conversational ball to her.

'Mariah is a very nice person.' She struggled with it gamely. 'No one is avoiding her . . . really. It's just . . . we don't seem to have all that much in common with her any more.'

Because Mariah still had a job? But Roz also had a job. And Nigel claimed to an independent financial consultant working from home—it could even be true, although I'd just as soon base my financial decisions on the flip of a coin as on any advice of his.

Before I could frame my next question, the doorbell rang. I caught the swift expression of relief crossing their faces: saved by the bell.

Could Evangeline have forgotten her keys? Perhaps she'd done so much shopping she couldn't manage the lock.

'You're back early.' I swung open the door. 'Oh, sorry. I thought it was—You're Hamish, aren't you?'

'Sorry to disturb you.' Hamish stood there, another young man with him. 'The Mortons told us they thought Nigel might be up here.'

'Yes, he is. Come in.' I stepped back. 'We were just having a drink. Do join us.'

'Thank you. Very kind of you. Have you met Sebastian? Sebastian Bolt, one of the partners in The Chummery, along with Eric and George. You'll probably meet them later.'

They marched in, literally in step, lightly swinging identical black leather attaché cases with brass-bound corners and combination locks, the sort that are supposed to look so executive-class and imposing, but all too often contain nothing more important than the morning newspaper and a packet of sandwiches.

I led them over to the cluster of furniture where Nigel and Roz sat watching us approach, our footsteps ringing out on the polished parquet floor of the foyer. The distance to the nearest rug had never seemed so far and I had to fight the feeling that I was about to break into a dance routine. Something inventive with bowlers, brollies and attaché cases and my two City gent chorus boys—with a *grande finale* of me, with a foot on each case, being raised up over their heads. And then, they'd probably drop me.

While everyone greeted each other, I escaped to the kitchen and rustled up more nibbles and drinks.

When I returned, the newcomers had claimed armchairs, pushed them closer to the sofa in a conversational grouping, and were looking around the enormous drawing-room with what seemed to be a certain amount of speculation in their eyes. They were probably wondering how much Jasper was soaking us for the rent. And perhaps wishing they'd seen us first.

Whatever they had been discussing, there was a sudden silence as I carried in the tray.

'Here, let me help you—' Hamish leaped to his feet and wrestled the tray from my hands, the glasses sliding as it tilted dangerously. We had just succeeded in righting it and accomplishing the transfer when the doorbell rang again. This time, it was Jasper. Whatever his original purpose for the visit, he seemed quite happy to put it on hold and join the others.

By the time Evangeline eventually returned, we had quite a party going. She let herself in and I wasn't aware she had arrived until I heard a familiar sound from the entrance.

'Huummmph!' She swept the room with a disapproving gaze, which came to rest on me. The disapproval deepened. 'I see you managed to think of something to do.'

'There you are!' I waved cheerfully, not at all averse to having her return to discover me surrounded by handsome young men. 'Someone get Evangeline a drink. She's had a hard day shopping.'

'Of course.' Nigel rushed to obey. 'What would you like?'

'Here, allow me—' Jasper leaped to take Evangeline's parcels and carry them to her room.

'Brandy.' Evangeline answered Nigel, faintly surprised that anyone had had to ask. 'Please.' She continued to gaze at me thoughtfully.

'Sit down, Evangeline,' I said. Those not already on their feet leaped up to offer her their seats. Evangeline bestowed an impartial gracious smile and took the nearest.

'Ah!' Nigel returned from the kitchen. 'I'm afraid there isn't any brandy. Can I offer you something else?'

'Don't be absurd.' Evangeline froze him with an icy glance. 'There was an unopened bottle out there this morning. Look again, dear boy.'

'Why don't you have a martini?' I suggested. It was a mistake.

'Oh?' Her eyes narrowed suspiciously at me. For a moment, I thought she was going to invite me to try to walk a straight line. 'And just what do you know about this missing bottle, Trixie?'

'It isn't missing. Er, actually, I brought it down to Sophie and Frederick.'

'You did *what?*'

'Well, I didn't feel up to baking something,' I explained. 'Not for a professional chef.' Out of the corner of my eye, I saw Roz nodding agreement.

'I will have a martini, dear boy.' Evangeline gave a martyred sigh. 'A strong one.' She closed her eyes and leaned back in her chair, a matriarch pushed to the limit of her endurance by thoughtless progeny.

Nigel darted off again with, I thought, a slightly puzzled expression.

'Are you all right, Evangeline?' Jasper was rash enough to ask.

'Since you ask—' Evangeline opened her eyes and glared at him—'I am not. I have been—' She paused portentously. 'I have been to the Post Office!' Her glare changed to accusation and she waited.

It didn't sound like a world-shaking revelation to me, but Jasper took only a moment of reflection before he stepped back, eyes widening in horror. 'Oh my God!'

'Well might you call upon Him.' Evangeline nodded grimly. 'And, if He doesn't strike you down, I am sorely tempted to do so myself.'

'I'm sorry. I'm so sorry. There was so much going on. I forgot.' Jasper was babbling apologies while the rest of us looked on, puzzled.

'Just what is this all about?' I asked. 'I seem to have skipped a chapter somewhere along the line.'

'You've been missing a few tricks lately, Trixie.' Evangeline didn't mind letting me know it. 'Haven't you noticed that we haven't had any mail in weeks?'

'Now that you mention it, we haven't.' I sent Jasper a

glare of my own. 'I didn't expect any in Whitby because I thought it would be waiting for us back here. But Jasper met us at the station and brought us to this place instead of St John's Wood and everything has been happening ever since and I forgot all about the mail.'

'I'm sorry,' Jasper said again. 'I forgot, too.'

'Well, where is it?' I looked from Evangeline's unforgiving face to Jasper's miserable one, and back again. 'You mean—?'

'Yes,' Evangeline said. 'Our friend here didn't bother to register a change of address with the post office. Heaven knows where all our mail has gone. Some of it was probably Returned to Sender. I don't know what they do with items without return addresses like postcards. You were getting quite a lot of postcards from Martha and the children, weren't you?'

'I *was*,' I said bitterly.

'I'm sorry.' Jasper turned his apologies to me. 'I'll see to it first thing in the morning.'

'You needn't bother,' Evangeline said. 'I've taken care of it myself. They were holding a couple of letters and postcards at the local post office and I've put a trace on the others to see if we can retrieve them. Everything else will come straight here now.' She gave Jasper an unpleasant smile and reached for her handbag. 'There's a letter for you from your grandparents.'

'Oh, great.' Jasper looked at the flimsy airmail envelope with its garish stamps as though it contained poison. She waggled it impatiently at him.

'Er, thanks.' He took it reluctantly.

'And postcards from the children—' She held them out to me.

'Thanks!' I snatched them eagerly and immersed myself in them.

'*Dear Trixie*—' This was from Viola. '*My hair is growing*

nice and long and Martha says I don't ever have to cut it again
unless I really truly want to. We are having a lovely time, but I
miss you.'

'Here you are.' Nigel arrived with Evangeline's drink just
as I raised my head to share the card with her, although
common sense told me she'd undoubtedly have read it
already.

Evangeline snatched at the drink as eagerly as I'd
snatched at the postcards and took a deep quaff. I watched
her face change as she stiffened and fought not to spit it
out. It obviously took a herculean effort of will to force
herself to swallow it. She took a deep breath and glared at
Nigel.

'This drink has no gin in it!' She transferred her glare to
me. 'Have you given away all the gin, too?'

The others stirred uneasily and tried to hide their glasses
as her accusing gaze swept over them. They were found
guilty of taking the drink, if not the food, out of her mouth.

'Gin? Ah! I'm sorry. You meant *that* kind of martini. I've
just given you the vermouth.'

'So I noticed.' Evangeline stretched out her hand and
emptied her glass into the nearest potted plant, which happened to be my orange tree.

'Ah! Sorry. I'll go and—' Nigel started for the kitchen.

'Don't bother.' Evangeline rose majestically. 'I have had
quite enough of this day. I shall retire to my room. I feel
one of my headaches coming on.'

'Ah! Perhaps we'd better leave.' Nigel could recognize a
cue when he heard one.

So could the others. They got to their feet.

'No, no, don't leave on my account,' Evangeline protested unconvincingly. 'Go on with your party. I'll be quite
all right—so long as you aren't too noisy.'

That did it, of course. Evangeline can be charming when

she wants to be, but when she doesn't, she can sure clear a room.

Her only equal was Mariah.

CHAPTER 11

'Trust you—' It was morning, but Evangeline wasn't in any better mood. 'Trust you to lack all discretion. I come home to find you hobnobbing with the suspects!'

'Wait a minute.' I got myself a cup of coffee and slumped down at the table. 'Nobody has even proved there's been a crime yet. Who says they're suspects?'

'That nice Superintendent Hee-Haw doesn't seem to have much doubt about it now. The medical examination proved I'm right. She was dead when she hit the water. From a violent blow to the head.'

'Wait a minute—' I am not at my brightest first thing in the morning, but I could see there was something fishy here. 'When did you talk to Heyhoe? Is that why you went to St John's Wood?'

'Don't be absurd.' Evangeline did not meet my eyes. 'I went to see about our mail. As long as I was in the neighbourhood, I thought I'd drop in on the Superintendent and find out if he'd made any progress.'

'But it isn't his case. He kept telling us that. This area is way out of his jurisdiction.'

'Nevertheless, he knew what was going on. I was sure he would. He was bound to take an interest in the case, since it came to light right under his nose, as it were.'

'Mmmm.' I doubted whether a busy policeman had the time to worry about someone else's cases. If he was taking an interest, it was probably because he hoped his colleagues would be able to pin it on Evangeline. Any maybe me.

'It was Nigel, of course,' Evangeline said with great certainty. 'In domestic murders, it's always the spouse who did it.'

'They weren't married,' I demurred. 'And Sandra seems to have been the breadwinner. Nigel won't even inherit—everything goes to Sophie. So he's a lot worse off.'

'How do you know Sophie gets everything?'

'The, er, subject came up while I was down visiting them yesterday. In fact, they had quite a fight about it. Nigel and Sophie, that is.'

'You *have* been busy.' She was not entirely disapproving. 'Tell me all.'

To my relief, the telephone rang just then. I was surprised to find Nigel on the other end of the line.

'Ah, good. You're up. We weren't sure you would be. Ah, I didn't wake you, did I?'

'No, we've been up for some time.' I tried to make the actual half-hour or so sound as though we'd been up since the crack of dawn.

'Ah, good. Then you won't mind if some of us come up now. We'd like to talk to you.'

'Come ahead.' Curiosity won out over the 'Hrrrmph'-ing noises Evangeline was making in the background. Instinct was obviously warning her that something was about to happen that she wasn't going to like. 'I'll make some more coffee.'

'Ah, that won't be necessary, but it's very kind of you. We'll be along in a moment.'

'We're about to have company,' I informed Evangeline, putting down the phone.

'At *this* hour?' She made it sound vaguely obscene. 'Who?'

'Nigel, for one. But he said "we", so there are probably more of them.'

Evangeline opened her mouth but before she could say anything, the doorbell rang.

'They can't be here already.' I went to answer it.

'They are.' Evangeline, more practical, had switched on the television monitor giving a view of the foyer outside. 'What's all that clutter they've got with them?'

'Good heavens!' I swung open the door and looked out on the enormous pile of furniture. They couldn't have moved all that since Nigel phoned. They must have moved it up here and piled it outside the door to wait until Nigel made his telephone call to us. What would they have done if I'd told him it was inconvenient to speak to them today? Would they have left everything piled in the foyer all day? What was it doing here anyway?

'Good morning,' they chorused. It was the same cast as last night, with a couple of additions. Non-speaking extras, I thought, as the two new men picked up a carved walnut chaise-longue with a peacock blue brocade upholstery and began to carry it past me into the penthouse.

'Just one moment!' Evangeline barred their way. 'What do you think you're doing?'

'Oh, I'm sorry.' Hamish had a large oil painting under his arm. 'We haven't told you. This is Eric and George—' They nodded glumly and walked past us with their burden.

'Perhaps, if we could come in—' Hamish executed a sidestep-and-slither, bypassing her neatly and carried his painting into the drawing-room where he set it down.

'It's just that we were all talking together after we left you last night.' Roz was carrying an elongated rosewood floor lamp carved in the shape of a dragon with a bulb and lampshade swinging from its mouth. 'And we thought, well, you have so much space here and you seem so sparsely furnished—'

'We thought we'd share a bit of our furniture with you. Ah! Purely as a loan—' Nigel wrestled with one of those

brass-bound teak military chests that were so fashionable
a few years ago.

I had given up. I stood back and let them carry their
offerings past me. I noted a fine antique rug, several large
Chinese vases, more oil paintings, a Glastonbury chair, and
items shrouded in thick protective wrappings that could
only be guessed at.

'How very sweet of you,' Evangeline cooed as the loot
went into the penthouse. I wondered if the donors realized
she had a touch of the late Queen Mary about her and
they'd be lucky if they got everything back at the end of
what they considered a term of loan.

The extras deposited the chaise-longue in front of the big
panoramic window, its back to the room so that its occu-
pant would be looking out at the view. Roz put the dragon
floor lamp behind it in a good position to light one's reading
matter. Someone spread the antique rug in front, Nigel set
the small low chest down where it could double as a coffee
table and—*voilà!*—suddenly that part of the drawing-room
had become a glorious little den with a view. I immediately
earmarked it for my own. My peacock blue dressing-gown
matched the chaise-longue, giving me clear proprietary
rights.

Meanwhile, I went into the kitchen to attend to the coffee
and, as I had feared, realized we did not have enough cups
for everybody. I asked Roz if we could borrow a couple
from her.

'Of course.' Her face lit up. 'I should have thought of it.
I have a dinner service I can lend you. I'll just get Nigel
to help me carry it.'

'No, wait!' I called after her. 'We don't need that much.
Just a few cups and saucers—' But she had already rushed
away, pulling Nigel with her.

The others were labouring mightily. I hadn't realized
they'd brought quite so much. Looking at the mass of

furniture being distributed around the penthouse, I feared
they had overdone their kindness. But I had to admit the
place looked a lot better.

Evangeline was supervising the hanging of the paintings.
(For someone who had objected to my socializing with the
'suspects', she had certainly swallowed her qualms when it
came to accepting favours from them.) Hamish had even
brought a hammer and picture hangers with him; he
seemed to have thought of everything. He worked with
enthusiasm, but his friends did not seem quite so enthusiastic. Maybe because they were doing the manual labour,
heaving the furniture about.

The one introduced as Eric, in fact, looked so disgruntled
that I began to wonder how much furniture they could
have remaining in their own flats. And why they were being
quite so sweet to us.

'Here we are!' Roz was back, panting slightly under the
weight of a large heavy carton. Nigel was right behind her,
carrying an even larger carton. They took them into the
kitchen, set them down on the table and Roz began un-
wrapping cups.

'Roz!' I caught my breath, recognizing the pattern. 'You
can't give us this. It's Wedgwood!'

'It's only a loan, remember.' She laughed. 'I know you'll
take good care of it.' And, the corollary hung in the air: if
we broke anything, we could afford to replace it.

'Nevertheless,' I said firmly, 'we can't accept this. We'll
use the cups for now and give them back to you when we've
finished.'

'Oh, but I *want* you to take it and use it.' Tears trembled
abruptly in her eyes. 'Please. It would be an honour—'

'Isn't that coffee ready yet?' Evangeline drifted into the
kitchen with a faintly puzzled frown and looked around.

'Coming right up, now that we've got some cups.' I gave

Roz a stern look. 'But we're not keeping them. You've all been generous enough as it is.'

'What's the matter?' Evangeline looked at us sharply.

'The Wedgwood service.' I gestured to it. 'It's too much. Even for a loan.'

'How charming.' Evangeline strolled over for a closer look. 'Just what we need for entertaining.'

'That's what I thought,' Roz said.

'It's too good,' I insisted.

'Nonsense!' Evangeline shot me a look that said nothing was too good for us—or for her, anyway. Then, for a wonder, she seemed to notice that the remark might have been a mite tactless.

'I mean—' She smiled engagingly at Roz. 'It's exactly what we would have bought for ourselves—if we'd had the time. It's very kind of you to give it to us.'

'*Lend* it to us,' I corrected warningly.

'In any case—' Evangeline frowned slightly, but continued in gracious mode—'it's extremely kind of you.'

'Actually,' Roz said nervously, 'I have to confess: I have an ulterior motive.'

I immediately began to feel better about the whole situation. Unlike Evangeline, I don't believe the world belongs at our feet just on general principles. A *quid pro quo* arrangement makes me more comfortable.

'Oh?' Evangeline arched an eyebrow at her. We both waited expectantly.

'I want to ask the most enormous favour of you—' She took a deep breath and plunged in. 'Both of you. So I've been organizing this—' she waved a hand, indicating the activity in the other rooms—'in the hope of putting you in such a good mood you won't refuse.'

We waited.

'You see, my sister works for the BBC and she was terribly excited when I told her you were moving in. She wants me to ask you if you'd be willing to appear on Desert Island Discs—'

'Together?' Evangeline managed to make it sound like *Haaandbaag?*

'Oh. Oh no. Separately, I think. Yes, it would be better that way. You're both such legends you can easily do a programme each. Oh, I do hope you will. She'll be so delighted—and she'll kill me if you don't.'

'Hmmm . . .' Evangeline hid her pleasure behind a thoughtful frown. 'I suppose I *could* fit it into my schedule. It would depend on the date.'

'Oh, they'll record it,' Roz said eagerly. 'You can do it any time and they'll broadcast it when they want to.'

'That's the favour to *you?*' I asked suspiciously. She must be pretty naïve to think we'd have to be bribed into appearing on the BBC. 'For your *sister?* And all these people are also loaning us their treasures because *your* sister—?'

'Ah!' Nigel stepped forward; he'd been so quiet I'd almost forgotten he was still there. 'Not exactly. We have our own ulterior motive. We want to make you so comfortable and happy here that you'll stay on. You may have noticed the place isn't fully occupied. Not many buildings around here are right now. The housing market is rather in the doldrums—only temporarily, I assure you.'

'Uh-huh.' I thought of those tattered advertising banners on the surrounding properties and wondered how long he considered temporary. Nothing had moved in years, from the look of them.

'So we thought we'd have a better—that is, Jasper would have a better—chance of selling the remaining flats if the place had more of an aura about it.' He bared his teeth at us briefly (What sharp teeth you have, Grandma.) 'Like glamorous neighbours.'

'Uh-huh.' Personally, I thought they'd have a better chance of selling if they did a few little things like putting the floors in the empty apartments and finishing the promised amenities. An underground garage, a swimming pool, a permanent caretaker and a gym would have more pulling power than a couple of superannuated actresses trailing clouds of glory from a bygone era.

Only the restaurant showed any signs of fulfilling the promises in the glossy brochure—and maybe not even that, if Sophie had a nervous breakdown. The way she kept fainting all over the place was not a good omen.

'I *knew* Jasper was using us as shills!' Evangeline said. 'I didn't know the rest of you were planning it, too.'

'This is a far cry from Las Vegas,' I said, 'but it looks like that's the general idea.'

'Ah! No, no, not exactly.' Nigel twitched unhappily. 'You misunderstand—'

'I believe we understand all too well,' Evangeline said.

'Perhaps we shouldn't blame them,' I said quickly, before she could get dramatic enough to suggest they take all the furniture away again. 'They mean well—'

'We're finished!' Hamish appeared in the doorway. 'Come and make sure everything is where you want it before you lose your moving men.'

'It looks marvellous.' I applauded. 'Absolutely terrific.'

'That refectory table—' Evangeline indicated it imperiously—'ought to be under that oblong painting to counterbalance it.'

'Eric!' Hamish snapped his fingers at the surlier of the non-speaking extras. 'You heard the lady. Under the painting!'

Eric mouthed something that looked fairly obscene at Hamish and gestured to his colleague. They heaved the heavy oak table into place. It did look better.

'That's a great improvement.' Hamish exhaled as though he had done all the heavy work himself. Eric and George were rubbing their backs and looking daggers at him.

'The place looks really good now,' Roz said with satisfaction.

'Almost too good.' Evangeline seemed to be edging
nearer to my point of view, but was still suspicious. 'You're
not planning to use this place as a Show Flat, are you?'

'No, no . . .'

'Never!'

'Certainly not!'

They denied it so vehemently and promptly as to re-
inforce the suspicion that that had been part of their original intention. Fortunately, Evangeline had forestalled it by
her question.

'We don't want strangers tramping through here.' Evangeline was slipping into a bad mood. I could see it coming.

'Oh no.' So could Roz. 'Neither do we. Want strangers
around the place, I mean. That's the last thing—'

One of the men cleared his throat meaningly and she
broke off.

'Jasper would never dream of using your penthouse as a
Show Flat,' Nigel said. 'He wouldn't dream of having you
disturbed.'

'He'd better not,' Evangeline muttered.

'Would one of you help me by carrying the tray?' I had
been getting it ready while the argument swirled around
me.

'Of course.'

'Certainly.' Nigel and Hamish almost collided, leaping
to respond to my request. I had the uneasy feeling that I
might have missed one of the undercurrents. They were
entirely too happy with the change of subject.

'Please—' Roz returned to her own problem as we followed the others into the now opulently-furnished drawing-
room. 'Is it all right for me to tell my sister to contact you?
You *are* willing to do the programme?'

'Oh well.' Evangeline made it sound like a great

concession on her part. 'I dare say we can manage it.'

CHAPTER 12

They had gulped their coffee and quite literally run. 'Have to get to the office,' was the excuse, even from Nigel who, we knew, did not have an office to go to. Roz tenderly loaded the china into the dishwasher and departed with the rest of them.

'As Gwenda would say, "Cwumbs!"' I wandered around the drawing-room admiring our new acquisitions. 'When these Yuppies loan things they don't do it by halves. Not a run-down cast-off in the lot.'

'Yuppies don't have second-hand items, they leave that to the peasants.'

'They do—but they call them antiques.' I ran my hand appreciatively over the smooth surface of a satinwood table. 'I just never knew they were so generous about throwing them around.'

'Lending something to us is hardly throwing it around.' Evangeline was on her high horse, but I had moved on and stopped listening.

It seemed to me that there were a lot more paintings hanging around the room than I had seen piled outside. I wondered if they all belonged to Hamish or whether some of the other chums from The Chummery had chipped in a few treasures. I began to prowl along the walls, examining them more closely. The long oblong painting above the refectory table was on the wall opposite the panoramic window, almost mirroring the scene outside. I did a double-take and closed in on it.

'Evangeline!' I squeaked—and found myself unable to say more. 'Evangeline—'

'What's the matter with you?' She glanced at me irritably. 'Don't stand there opening and shutting your mouth like a stranded fish. What is it?'

'It— I think it's a Canaletto!'

'Nonsense!' She was at my side before I had gasped out the final syllable. 'You mean '*After* Canaletto', or possibly "*School of*"—' Her nose was almost touching the canvas.

'Don't breathe on it!' I was feeling faintly hysterical. 'You might damage it.'

'Idiocy!' Evangeline breathed, but she turned her head and breathed out into the open air.

A painting farther along the wall caught her eye, a rather jolly music hall scene, and she moved to examine it. I joined her, standing back to absorb the full impression. I'd seen that style before . . . perhaps in a museum . . .

'Walter Sickert, I believe,' Evangeline murmured.

'Sure it's not "*School of*"?' I could not resist the gibe.

'I'm not sure of anything at this point,' Evangeline said, 'except that we've had some very valuable paintings foisted on to us.' She moved away and began circling some of our other new acquisitions.

'It's no good your inspecting the furniture,' I said. 'You know you wouldn't know a Biedermeier from a bedpan.'

'I once played Florence Nightingale, remember.'

'OK, but you still don't know anything about furniture.'

'I know enough to suspect that, good as it is, it isn't nearly so valuable as the paintings.'

Even I knew that. Furniture never was. You often read about tens of millions of dollars being paid for one painting; you could furnish a whole streetful of houses for that and still have something left over.

From the kitchen, the dishwasher gave a demented whine and shut itself off, recalling me to more mundane matters.

'You can hang around here and assess the loot, if you want,' I said. 'But I'm calling for a taxi and going out for some supplies. We've gone through just about everything I bought the other day and it's time for another trip to the supermarket.'

'Do you know?' She surprised me. 'I think I'll come with you.'

We were closing the door when she surprised me again. 'Just a minute, Trixie.' She brushed at my hair in a gesture that was almost affectionate until—

'Ouch!' I rubbed at the site of the pain. She'd pulled several hairs out. 'What did I do? Why are you mad at me now?'

'I'm not.' She bent and inserted one of the hairs well below the doorknob as she closed the door and locked it. If you weren't looking for it, you'd never know it was there.

'That's better.' Evangeline straightened. 'Now we'll know if anyone enters during our absence. I still think they're planning to use it as a Show Flat; hence all the luxury furnishings to impress prospective buyers. But they won't get away with it. We can catch them out by using this simple precaution whenever we leave the flat empty.'

'Next time use your own hair,' I said bitterly.

Going through a supermarket with Evangeline was worse than having a child in tow. Shopping took twice as long and we wound up with three times as much as I'd have bought on my own. It didn't improve matters when she got into a bad temper at being stuck in the queue for so long and took it out on the cashier, who wasn't in the best of moods herself. I tried to pretend I'd never seen her before in my life, but blew my cover when I had to pay for every-thing on my credit card. I made a mental note never to get caught up in that cashier's line again.

It was a silent taxi ride back. We had almost reached

our turning when Evangeline's elbow sank into my ribs. I moved away impatiently, but she did it again.

'Look!' she said. 'Over there! I *knew* we were under police surveillance!'

I looked, just in time to see a tall thin man glance impatiently at his watch, turn and disappear around a corner, conspicuously fed up with waiting for someone.

'He doesn't look like a policeman to me.'

'Plainclothes, of course.' Evangeline snorted. 'And how about that corny routine of looking-at-his-watch-shaking-his-head-and-giving-up-waiting-for-the-person-who-was-so-late? As though anyone would choose to meet someone around here. He knew we spotted him and was making his getaway.'

'Maybe.' I still wasn't convinced.

'He was hanging around here yesterday, too. You didn't go out, so you didn't see him.'

'Yes, but—' I lowered my voice, glancing at the taxi-driver. The glass partition seemed to be closed and the driver was keeping his attention on the road. 'But why should the police be watching now? *If* Sandra was murdered, it happened weeks ago. And there's been a lot of wind and rain to wash any clues away. Any trail would be dead cold; there can't be anything left to discover. Watching the building would just be a waste of time.'

'Watching the *suspects*.' Evangeline was not going to give up her theory easily. 'He *must* be. There's no other reason for anyone to loiter around here. There's nothing to see, nothing to do. Mark my words, he's watching the sus—'

'Here we are.' The taxi-driver spoke loudly and I realized he had pulled up in front of the entrance a couple of minutes ago.

'Hmmmmmph!' Evangeline didn't like the implication that we had been too busy arguing to notice we had arrived.

'Pay the man, Trixie.' She opened the door and stalked off.

'And don't overtip!'

'Dunno, love.' The driver shook his head sympathetically. 'Maybe I was wrong. The Embankment might be an improvement.'

'I remember you!' I recognized him now. 'You've driven us before. Out from the West End. What were you doing at the supermarket cab stand?'

'Live out this way, don't I?' He got out and helped me unload the bags of shopping. 'Sometimes I don't fancy the long haul into town with an empty cab. Supermarket's always good for local fares. Shoppers come out on the bus, but they're too loaded up to struggle back on it. You should see their faces light up when they see us waiting on the rank.'

'Trixie!' Evangeline called shrilly. 'Are you going to stand there gossiping all day? Come along!'

'You didn't ought to have to put up with that,' the cabbie muttered. 'Here—' He fished in one of his pockets and brought out a grubby business card. 'You need a break? You call me and I'll pick you up and ride you around a bit. Don't worry—no charge.'

'Oh—' I consulted the card quickly. 'Oh, Eddie.' I was touched. 'Thank you, but honestly—'

'Trixie!' Evangeline gestured imperiously. 'Come here at once! I can't find my keys!'

'That's it!' I sighed. 'I've got to go.'

'She's got no right to push you around like that—just because you're down on your luck.' He ground the gears and started off. 'You call me, mind.'

'First the suspects, now the servants!' Evangeline watched me struggle with all the bags. 'I do wish you'd mingle with a better class of people. Why don't you go into the West End and pick up a Producer? That might do us some good.'

'I've already got a Producer in the Family,' I said coldly. 'Anyway, a taxi-driver isn't a servant.'

'A tradesman?' Evangeline paused and considered the exact classification. 'At any rate, he's plying for hire. And your vaunted Producer might as well be a marble statue for all the use he is to us. How long are they going to stay away? How long can a honeymoon last? You'd think they'd be sick of the sight of each other by now.'

'Maybe that's the story of *your* honeymoons, but this is Martha's first. She's enjoying it and I hope it lasts her lifetime.'

'Hmmmmph!'

'*Some* people manage it.' I'd moved all the bags to the top step while Evangeline just stood and watched me. No wonder people thought I was some sort of slavey.

'Don't worry about helping me with the bags,' I said pointedly as I unlocked the front door and swung it open. 'I can manage quite well and I *am* younger than you.'

That did it. She snatched up the two nearest carrier bags and staggered over to the lifts, left them there and came back for more. Working silently, we both ferried nearly everything to the lift.

'I'll leave the last trip to you,' Evangeline said. 'As you're younger and stronger.'

I might have known it. The three bags that were left were so heavy I could hardly lift even one of them—and they all clanked. We were not going to run out of booze again in a hurry, no matter how many bottles I gave away.

'Please let me help.' A soft, pleasant female voice spoke behind me. I turned.

'Why, Mariah, how kind of you.' I hastily caught up the lightest bag and started across the foyer.

Behind me, I heard the clanking of bottles and a muffled gasp as Mariah grappled with more than she had bargained for. Steadfastly, I walked straight ahead and didn't look back until I had set down my burden in front of the lift. Evangeline had pushed the button to summon the 'Local' and clearly considered that she had done her share by doing that.

Mariah was staggering only slightly as, a bag in each hand and her attaché case under her arm, she crossed the foyer to us.

'Just put them inside,' Evangeline directed, 'and then help Trixie load the others.' She paused thoughtfully. 'And perhaps you'd be kind enough to come up with us and help us unload. After all—' she shot me a nasty look—'you're younger and stronger than we are.'

'Of course.' Mariah followed us meekly into the lift, although I noticed she clutched her attaché case defensively, holding it between herself and Evangeline like a shield.

But Evangeline had nothing more to say for the moment. We rode upwards in silence, but I could feel Evangeline thinking and it made me nervous.

'Here we are.' The lift doors opened and Evangeline skipped out before anyone could suggest she take a shopping-bag. 'I'll go and put the kettle on. You *will* stay for a cup of tea, my dear?'

'Me?' Mariah looked over her shoulder.

'Or something stronger, if you prefer.'

'Me?' Having discovered no one behind her, Mariah was now looking around the foyer. 'You're inviting *me?*'

She sounded as though she couldn't believe it. If I hadn't seen the way the others avoided her, I'd have thought she had the world's worst inferiority complex. As it was, it was obviously a novelty for anyone to put up with her presence, let alone actively seek it.

'Hurry up.' Evangeline swung the door open with only the briefest glance to make sure the hair was still in place. 'Don't stand there dreaming.'

By the time we had carried all the bags into the kitchen, Evangeline had drinks poured, abandoning any nonsense about kettles and tea. However, after unpacking and storing all the supplies away, we were ready for something stronger.

Mariah accepted her drink gratefully and sank down in a corner of the sofa. It wasn't until she'd taken a few reviving sips that she began to look around. Her eyes grew thoughtful.

'You may recognize a few items.' I figured she had already and was busy putting two and two together. 'Some of the neighbours thought our furnishings were a bit sparse, so they've loaned us their surplus pieces. They're so kind and welcoming—'

I broke off as something flashed in the depths of her eyes and I remembered they weren't so kind or welcoming to *her*.

'So sweet of them.' Evangeline stepped in to cover my confusion. 'And such a bright idea.'

'Oh yes.' Mariah's voice was flat and emotionless. 'They're full of bright ideas.'

Evangeline and I didn't quite look at each other. We waited hopefully, but Mariah wasn't prepared to expand on her statement. She continued to look around the drawing-room, obviously able to name the real owner of every one of our bits of borrowed luxury.

That meant that once she must have been on much better terms with the other residents—otherwise, how would she know? And what had gone wrong with the relationships?

'Isn't this pleasant?' Evangeline leaned back and smiled innocently. 'Trixie and I pride ourselves that we like to know our neighbours, but we hardly ever see you around. You must be a very busy young woman.'

'Yes.' Mariah sighed faintly. 'I seem to have been working overtime since I can't remember when.'

That certainly made a change from most of the others in
the building. Evangeline leaned forward for the kill.

'And just what do you—'

The doorbell interrupted her. I answered it to find Nigel
and Hamish on the doorstep.

'—do?' I heard Evangeline finish behind me, but it was
too late.

'What are you doing here?' Nigel demanded of Mariah.
Hamish wasn't pleased to see her, either. They hovered in
the entranceway, glowering at her.

'Don't worry.' Mariah drained her glass and stood up.
'I was just leaving.'

'Oh, but—' Evangeline's protest went unnoticed; for
once, she was not the centre of attention.

'You'd better not—' Hamish moved forward with a
vague air of menace.

'Don't worry,' Mariah said again. 'I haven't seen a
thing.' She sidestepped them, moving rapidly, and I heard
the door close behind her.

'What was that all about?' Evangeline demanded.

'What all?' Nigel tried to act as though he didn't understand. Hamish ignored the question.

'Why are you persecuting that poor young woman?'

'*Us?* Persecuting *her?* Nigel gave a hollow laugh. Hamish
trod on his foot and he shut up, a bland, improbably innocent expression spreading over his face.

'And what hasn't she seen?' Evangeline persisted.

'Who knows? Practically anything, I should think.'
Hamish gave her a ravishing smile. 'Let's talk about you.
You're so much more interesting than dull old Mariah.'

'Well . . .' Evangeline bridled, as she was expected to.

Hamish smiled the self-satisfied smile of a thousand
unwary directors who thought they'd handled the empty-
headed, egocentric little actress brilliantly. Get them talking
about themselves and they'll forget everything else.

But he didn't know Evangeline. She was going to let him get away with it—for the moment. She'd come back at him when he least expected it.

'Do sit down,' I suggested, deciding to play the silly little woman myself, since that was what Hamish seemed to think of us. 'You make me feel uncomfortable, looming over us like that.' I even batted my eyelashes at him.

'Thank you.' He fell for it, just as I knew he would. He and Nigel took chairs and seated themselves, both looking around casually but sharply.

'You know,' Nigel said, 'you ought to be more careful who you let in here. Not to put too fine a point on it, there are undesirables around who might take advantage.'

'You can't mean Mariah!' Evangeline pretended to be shocked. 'Such a sweet young girl, I thought. I'm just sorry we haven't had a chance to see more of her.'

'Ah! No! No!' Nigel was genuinely shocked. 'You don't want to do that.'

'Why not?'

'Ah! Well . . .' For a moment, I thought he was going to try telling us that we were too young and innocent to know. Or that the details were too sordid for our delicate ears.

But he looked at us closely and realized that wouldn't wash. In our combined years in Hollywood, we'd seen and heard a lot more than he ever would.

'Ah! Er . . .' He settled back in his chair and looked to Hamish to bail him out.

Hamish rose slowly and walked across to his Sickert. He studied it thoughtfully, decided it was hanging slightly crooked and made a minor adjustment, checked the new alignment by holding his hands up in front of his face in a framing gesture, then returned to his chair, smiling blandly.

The subject was closed; in fact, it had never been opened. The technique probably worked a treat in tricky business meetings.

'Do you mind if I smoke?' he asked.

'I don't care if you burn!' Evangeline said tartly.

'Oh, that's a good one,' he chortled. He honestly seemed never to have heard that old chestnut before. Maybe he hadn't. It went back to the early days of smoking before some bright spark in advertising got the idea of enlarging the market by running ads with wide-eyed young beauties simpering at their big strong men: 'Blow some my way, it smells so good.'

Hamish lit his cigarette with what was probably a solid gold lighter, inhaled deeply and—perhaps it was thought transference—exhaled right in Evangeline's direction. Her eyes narrowed.

'Tell us, dear boys,' she cooed. 'To what do we owe the honour of this visit? You've done so much for us already that we're feeling quite spoiled. Have you now come to place your chariots at our disposal?'

Hamish winced involuntarily. That one had got him right between the eyes.

'Ah, what?' Nigel didn't get it at all.

'Your Rolls-Royce, dear,' Evangeline elucidated. 'Your Mercedes, your Jaguar, your BMW, your chariot, your automobile, your car.' She paused and looked at them innocently before aiming right between the eyes again. 'You *do* have a car, don't you?'

'Ah! Well!' Nigel stiffened and began babbling. 'We do. I mean, I do. He does. But we've had a bit of car trouble lately. A lot of trouble, actually. They're . . . they're unusable right now.'

'What Nigel means,' Hamish said smoothly, 'is that our cars are in the garage being repaired. And not just our cars. We've had a lot of trouble with cars around here . . .' He trailed off, perhaps recognizing the echo of Nigel's plaint.

'Not accidents, I hope.' Evangeline looked concerned, probably because this meant she didn't know where her next ride was coming from. '*All* of you can't have had crashes . . . can you?'

'Ah! Not crashes, no—' Nigel began, but Hamish took over.

'Sabotage,' Hamish said, with a dark look at Nigel. 'You may have noticed the graffiti on the front of the building. Jasper has had it removed a couple of times, but it keeps reappearing.'

YUPPIE SCUM OUT! Yes, it was rather noticeable. We nodded encouragingly.

'The locals have it in for us,' Hamish continued. 'They hate all the redevelopment. They think we're depriving them, in some way, of housing that would otherwise be theirs. All nonsense, of course. These warehouses have been standing burnt-out and empty since the Blitz; they had plenty of time to do something with them if they'd wanted to.'

'They wanted other people to do it,' Nigel said. 'The Council, the Government, anyone but themselves.'

'I don't suppose they had the money,' I said softly. 'This doesn't look like a very wealthy area—once you get away from the redevelopment along the river.'

'Anyway—' Hamish shrugged off my comment. 'They have a grudge against us—and they take it out on us any way they can. The graffiti on the building, the occasional stone hurled through a window, and the cars—especially the cars. They seem to resent them as much as the building.'

'It's Jasper's fault,' Nigel complained. 'If he'd only built the underground garage first, we wouldn't have had any of this trouble. But no, he had to get the luxury flats done first, so we've had to park our cars unprotected out in the open where—'

'Where they've had a considerable amount of damage done to them,' Hamish finished for him.

'Roz's car seemed all right,' I said. 'She gave us a lift to the supermarket a few days ago.'

'Ah! Roz!' Nigel twitched irritably. 'Roz was one of the first to move in. She was able to rent a lock-up garage nearby. She and—' he almost spat the name—'Mariah!'

'It's all most unfortunate,' Hamish said quickly. 'It means most of us are without proper transport for the time being. We're pressuring Jasper for completion of the underground garage in the basement, as promised, but—' He shrugged. 'Jasper has his problems, too.'

'So it would seem,' Evangeline said drily.

'Actually, that was what we wanted to warn you about,' Hamish said. 'Some of the locals are more aggressive than the others. They lurk about outside and try to gain entrance by pushing in behind you when you open the door. If one ever got in and hid in the building—' he shuddered—'and opened the door to the others after dark, they could do an appalling amount of damage before they were discovered. If they were discovered . . .'

'Lurking . . .' I said thoughtfully, carefully not looking at Evangeline.

'He's been seen around again lately,' Hamish said, rising. 'So we thought we'd better warn you. You can't be too careful who you let in.'

They left rapidly, before we could bring the conversation round to Mariah again.

CHAPTER 13

'I told you he didn't look like a policeman,' I said as soon as the door had safely closed behind them.

'There's one way to find out for certain.' Evangeline

marched purposefully to the phone. 'If Superintendent Tee-Hee doesn't know, then he can find out for us.'

'Uh-huh.' I could imagine how pleased Heyhoe would be to do a little errand like that and decided I wasn't going to hang around to listen. I gathered up the dirty glasses, took them into the kitchen and pottered about in there for a suitable interval after I heard Evangeline slam the phone down.

'Of all the impertinence!' she fumed as I came back into the room. 'He said (a) it was none of my business, (b) we weren't important enough to have a stakeout and (c) it wasn't—'

'His jurisdiction,' I chorused along with her. 'Well, it isn't. He's told you that before.'

'He did say,' she admitted grudgingly, 'that he might ring up and check the position with the local constabulary, but not to hold my breath waiting.'

'Uh-huh.' It was more likely that he *had* told her to hold her breath—and he'd call back some time around the middle of next week.

'That man has a filthy temper.' Evangeline was still aggrieved. 'I don't know how he got where he is if he goes around treating the public like that. He ought to be more—'

The telephone rang and, as she was nearest, she answered. I saw her expression change from annoyance to satisfaction and back to annoyance again.

'What do you mean, what have we done now?' she demanded. 'We haven't done anything. I don't know what you're talking about.'

'Who is it?' I asked. She shook her head impatiently.

'Account for our movements today? Of course we can. We had friends in for coffee this morning, we did some shopping at a supermarket and then came back here and had a few more friends in for drinks—'

'Heyhoe?' I asked. He was the only person who'd be asking questions like that. And I didn't like where the questions seemed to be heading.

'Witnesses?' Evangeline whooped indignantly. 'Proof?'

'There was the cashier at the supermarket,' I prompted. 'She'd remember us.' She'd never forget us. It didn't seem like such a bad thing now. 'And the taxi-driver. Why does Heyhoe want to know?'

'Why do you want to know?' Evangeline repeated into the phone. 'What? There's just been a report of a *what*?'

Heyhoe seemed to speak at length and with considerable fervour. Evangeline went pale and held the phone away from her ear. When she finally replaced the phone in its cradle and turned to me, she hardly needed to tell me.

Already, in the distance, we could hear the sirens of approaching police cars.

The question now was: Who?'

We could reasonably assume that Mariah, Nigel and Hamish were safe, as we had seen them so recently. That still left a lot of inhabitants unaccounted for.

'Jasper?' I gasped. Everyone seemed to be pretty annoyed with him, but annoyed enough to kill? How would we ever face his grandparents again if anything had happened to him?

'Lazlo?' Evangeline had her own nomination. 'Someone's been out to get him. If they couldn't cripple him financially, perhaps they've settled for killing him.'

We stared at each other in consternation for one long moment, then turned and hurled ourselves through the door and across the foyer, each banging on a different door.

No one answered either door. We looked at each other.

'They can't both . . .' Evangeline trailed off. They could. And we knew it.

'No, it can't be.' I was calmer now and thinking

rationally. The sirens had stopped a couple of minutes ago. 'If anything had happened up here, we'd hear the lifts bringing the police up by now. It's something on one of the lower floors.'

'Sophie?' Evangeline wondered. 'Could she have been brooding and got upset enough to do . . . something silly?'

'I wouldn't have thought she was the suicidal type. Besides, she still has Frederick.'

'And she seems about to inherit a goodly amount of money.' Evangeline obviously considered that more of a comfort than Frederick.

'Wait—' Evangeline listened intently. 'The lift is starting up now.'

She was right; I could hear the low whine as the lift laboured upwards. They had chosen the wrong one.

'Maybe we ought to go back inside and not be caught hovering around out here. If that lift breaks down again, they aren't going to arrive in the best of moods.' Already the pitch of the whine had changed to downright complaint and then it stopped altogether.

'Mmmm, yes.' Evangeline began moving.,

We retreated as far as our entrance hall and didn't quite shut the door behind us. We'd hear the voices when the lift finally made it. Then we could go out, acting innocent, and maybe learn what was going on.

Only . . . 'I hear voices already.' I looked at Evangeline. 'It sounds as though they're in our kitchen.'

'Nonsense! They can't be.' But Evangeline looked worried. 'They couldn't have got past us without our seeing them.'

'Maybe, but someone's out there.' I headed for the kitchen and she followed.

'You see—' She was right, the kitchen was empty. But the voices were clearer, although not so clear that we could distinguish actual words. There was just a general rumble of male voices and a certain amount of crashing around. 'The abyss—' I realized. We crossed to the door leading to the vast drop of the unconstructed flats-to-be and opened it cautiously.

It was like looking down on a film set from one of the catwalks high above. The swarming figures were circling a spread-eagled body on the floor so far below. It seemed to be male and, even if it hadn't been face down, we couldn't have identified it from this height and distance.

As we watched, someone began setting up lights and someone else moved in with a camera. The very familiarity of watching a camera man taking stills was soothing—until we remembered that this wasn't a film in production. This was in deadly earnest.

'Too thin to be Lazlo,' Evangeline murmured with relief. I suspected she had Lazlo marked down as a prospective backer for our play—when we found one.

'Shhhh . . .' If the police looked up and discovered they had an audience, they wouldn't be pleased.

We watched in silence for a few minutes until we saw one of the policemen begin twitching and looking around uneasily. Perhaps he could feel someone watching him, or perhaps our partly-opened door was creating some sort of draught. He hadn't thought to look upwards yet.

I signalled to Evangeline and we withdrew, closing the door silently behind us. We might want to use our observation post again and it was as well not to draw any attention to it.

'I think—' Evangeline surveyed the now-closed door with dissatisfaction—'I think we ought to go downstairs and see what we can find out.'

'It sure wasn't Jasper, either.' I felt free to talk now, although I still kept my voice low. 'He wouldn't be caught dead in a sweater like that. I mean—'

'I know what you mean. And furthermore, Jasper would

have known better than to walk out of a door that opened on to empty space.' Her lips tightened. 'No one knows better just where all the death traps in this building are located. Let's get down there and find out who it *is*.'

Both lifts were in use, so we turned to the stairs. The voices grew louder as we descended. But, more disturbingly, there was another sound to be heard in the stairwell, one that obviously could not be heard by the police working around the body or it would have been traced to its source and investigated.

Someone—impossible to tell whether it was a man or a woman—was sobbing broken-heartedly.

'We'll start with the ground floor, I think,' Evangeline decided as we stopped for a rest, 'and see what sort of activity is going on there.'

'The other activity seems to have stopped.' Perhaps the person had heard us talking and realized that sound travels both ways. We could no longer hear the wrenching sobs.

'It couldn't—' A horrible thought struck me. 'That body couldn't be Frederick?'

'The sooner we get there—' Evangeline started determinedly down the next flight of stairs—'the sooner we'll find out.'

That is, if the policemen would tell us. I stopped myself from saying it aloud as I followed her down the stairs. There was no point in borrowing trouble, we were soon going to have a plateful.

A chill draught had begun making itself felt and I was not surprised when we reached the ground floor to find the front door wedged wide open.

Two police cars and an ambulance could be seen in the street outside and, as we strolled casually into the lobby, a man in plainclothes walked briskly past us, carrying the sort of satchel usually identified as a doctor's bag. Two uniformed men struggled in his wake, grappling with some sort of equipment.

'Excuse me—' Evangeline smiled sweetly at them all— 'but what on earth is going on here?'

They ignored her and disappeared into the lift. There was a muffled crash as the door tried to close on some of the equipment.

'Well!' It didn't take much to send Evangeline into a huff and she was off.

'Not very polite,' I agreed placatingly. 'And not very safe, either, leaving the front door open like that.'

Evangeline sniffed. 'Not many people would dare to walk in with all these police around.'

'I should think it would be a good time. The police won't know all the people who live in the building yet. And the residents can't possibly know who's a legitimate plain-clothes copper and who isn't. Half the neighbourhood could sneak in here now and hide away, biding their time to do some mischief.'

'Perhaps we ought to close the door.' I had made Evangeline uneasy. 'There's no notice to say we shouldn't.'

'If they don't like it, we can always tell them they can't freeze the place out just because there's been a—'

'We don't *know* what's happened here yet, but I think it's high time somebody told us.' Evangeline looked around restlessly, but there was no one to tell us a thing.

We were struggling with the doors and had just kicked the wedge aside when a wild-eyed Jasper took the steps with one bound and burst into the entranceway.

'What's the matter?' he cried. 'Why is the place swarming with police?'

'I've no idea.' Evangeline surveyed him coolly and a glint appeared in her eyes. 'However, you're the owner of this building and they'll have to tell *you*.' She slipped a hand through his arm. 'Come along and we'll get to the bottom of this.'

Shuddering slightly at the picture her words had brought to mind: the body lying at the bottom of the long drop, I took Jasper's other arm, determined not to be left out.

Together we steered him towards the lift and Evangeline knew which button to press. The doors reopened on a scene of uniformed activity clustered around an open door leading on to the floor where the body lay.

'What's going on in there?' Jasper craned his neck to see. Evangeline and I displayed a ladylike reticence; we already knew.

'We'll be with you in just a minute, sir,' one of the men said indifferently. The others ignored us. They were good at that. I was beginning to feel like the Invisible Woman.

'Tell them you own the building,' Evangeline prodded. 'You have a right to know. Demand to see the man in charge.'

'Who *is* in charge?' Jasper demanded. 'This is my building. I have a right to know what's going on here.'

'That's right.' Evangeline nodded approval, she liked someone who could take directions. 'Don't let them brush you off.'

I nodded, too, but remained silent. The group of policemen were starting to become aware of us as possible troublemakers. We got a few impatient glances and a couple of frowns but, in general, they radiated the impression that they were too caught up in their work of utmost importance to waste time on dithering civilians. That suited me just fine.

Evangeline was impatient, however. 'Will you kindly—' She went into her *grande dame* manner. '*Kindly* inform your superior that we wish to speak to him.'

'That's right.' Jasper continued to follow her lead. 'Who's in charge here, anyway.'

'Inspector Crichton, sir.'

'*Not* the Admirable Crichton,' Evangeline murmured.

'Oh, you know him?' The constable looked at her with more interest.

'How could I forget our long run in the Broadway revival?' Evangeline preened. 'Not to mention the eight-month triumphal tour through the boondocks.'

'Ummm.' The constable looked puzzled. 'Perhaps I'd better tell him you're here.' He melted away rapidly.

Evangeline released Jasper's arm and began edging closer to the group in conference. I found that, by shifting my own position slightly, I could almost see beyond the doorway. If it wasn't for the policemen in between.

Abruptly, they all stood to one side and I caught a glimpse of the sprawled body in the middle of the floor. The blood and the crumpling of the limbs hadn't been so noticeable from our previous catwalk view. I closed my eyes and, when I opened them again, the Inspector had materialized in front of me.

'I understand one of you owns this building,' he said.

'I do,' Jasper admitted in a faint voice. He had obviously seen the body, too.

'Are you Inspector Crichton?' Evangeline couldn't stay out of it for one minute.

Not that I blamed her for asking the question. He looked about twelve years old. Well, maybe fourteen. I know policemen are supposed to be looking younger every year— but Inspectors?

'Then you know everyone in the building, sir?' He did not bother to answer Evangeline directly. With an expertise that was obviously born of long practice, he whipped out his identification and held it in front of Evangeline's face, while he continued to give his full attention to Jasper.

'Yes, yes, of course, I do. They're—' Jasper faltered, his

eyes turned towards that doorway again. 'They're all my friends.'

'Then you wouldn't mind identifying the body.' It was not a question. He repocketed his warrant card abstractedly, still without a direct look at Evangeline, and began manœuvring Jasper towards the doorway.

'Oh, er, um . . .' Not surprisingly, Jasper was reluctant. 'Isn't that the job of the next of kin?'

'Until we know who it is, we can't find the next of kin,' Inspector Crichton said reasonably.

'Oh yes, of course.' Unhappily, Jasper allowed himself to be led away. We tried to go along with him, but Inspector Crichton somehow got in our way and hustled Jasper through the doorway, muttering something to the other policemen as he went past. We found our way blocked.

'He'll only be a minute, madam,' one of the policemen said. 'He'll be right back.'

'We were just—' Evangeline tried to look past him.

'Shut the door,' an abrupt voice in the background commanded. The others stepped back into the room and closed the door behind them.

'Impudent brat!' Evangeline fumed. 'He ought to be home oiling his roller-skates!'

'He'll probably end up as the head of New Scotland Yard.' We'd seen these types before. Every once in a while Nature throws off one of these sports: perpetual adolescents, at least in looks, from the age of fourteen to about forty-five. They can go through life paying half fare for everything, but have to fight with ID cards to buy a drink. Quite a few of them used to gravitate to Hollywood where they could feature endlessly in teenage B pictures. Inspector Crichton seemed to be in better shape than a lot of them; at least, his voice had broken.

For the smart ones, it carried an inbuilt advantage: people underestimated them. The 'grown-ups' would tell them to go pedal their kiddie karts and forget about them, little realizing that the 'kiddies' were busily undermining their position and authority—until the day they found themselves out of a job and wondering what had hit them. More than one studio executive could testify to that.

'They make me nervous.' Evangeline had obviously just taken a short trip down Memory Lane, too. 'You never know what they're thinking—or doing. I don't trust them.'

'This one's a policeman,' I reminded her.

'Even worse. I wonder if he's bent?'

'Shhh!' The door had opened again and Jasper walked over to us unsteadily. He was faintly green around the gills and seemed to be swallowing a lot.

Inspector Crichton walked slightly behind him, ready to catch him if he fainted.

'What have you done to poor Jasper?' Evangeline demanded.

'He'll be all right, madam. It takes some of them that way, identifying a body. You can take him back to his flat now. Someone will be along to take his statement presently.'

'What about us?' Evangeline was feeling left out. 'Don't you want to ask us any questions?'

'Why? Can you tell us anything?' Inspector Crichton gave her a peculiar look. It made me suspect that he had had a long conversation with Superintendent Heyhoe at some point.

'Anything concrete, that is,' he added. 'That could be used in evidence.' No doubt about it, Heyhoe had really burned his ears about us. 'Think it over carefully,' he said. 'Someone will take a statement from you . . . eventually.'

'I must say you're very casual about it. My good friend, Detective-Superintendent Heyhoe would never— Watch what you're doing, Trixie! That was my foot!'

And it was in her mouth, as usual.

'Look at Jasper,' I said hastily. 'I think we'd better get him upstairs right away.'

Evangeline looked and, for once, agreed with me.

'Upstairs,' she ordered. 'Brandy—quickly!'

CHAPTER 14

'I'll be all right.' Jasper shuddered and took another sip. 'Just give me a minute or two. It was the shock of seeing— I'll be all right.'

'Who was it?' Evangeline couldn't wait.

'Was it Frederick?' I was pretty anxious myself.

'Frederick? No. What made you think of him?'

'Oh, I don't know.' I could not tell him of the frantic sobs we had heard. 'Maybe because Sophie just lost her sister. Things run in threes—and that would have made the second for Sophie.'

'God! The ideas you have!' Jasper shuddered again and finished his brandy in one go. When he stopped gasping, he looked around for a refill.

'How about Nigel?' Evangeline asked, with slightly less concern. 'He lost Sandra, too.'

'No, it wasn't Nigel.' The way Jasper looked at us made me feel we were squatting around a smoking cauldron waiting for the Thane of Cawdor to come over the hill. All that was missing was the third witch—and maybe the eye of newt.

'It was Eric!' Jasper realized he'd have no peace until he told us. 'My God! Poor Eric! He was just beginning to see daylight financially. And now this!'

'Who?' Both Evangeline and I momentarily drew a blank on that.

'Eric Pommeroy. From The Chummery. You don't know him.'

'One of the non-speaking extras,' I recognized, and explained to Evangeline. She nodded comprehension.

'What?' It was Jasper's turn to be at a loss.

'We sort of met him, just to say "how-do-you do",' I told Jasper. 'He helped the others move the stuff in here.'

'Move? What stuff?' Jasper looked around and stiffened as his gaze fell on what was evidently a familiar object. 'Oh! Oh, I see.' He turned slowly, taking in every item.

'It was their idea.' I began apologizing; I wouldn't hurt Jasper's feelings for the world. 'We were quite happy with the furniture you provided, Jasper. It was the others who thought the place looked, well, a bit sparsely furnished. They brought all these things in of their own accord. We didn't ask them—'

'They were right.' Slowly, Jasper began nodding approval. 'The place does look the better for it. Yes, it was a good idea.' He laughed abruptly.

'A brilliant idea, in fact.' He went on laughing. I began to wonder if he could stop. The hysterical reaction of being forced to identify the body of his friend was setting in.

'Have a drop more brandy.' Evangeline hastily refilled his glass. 'Sit down and take a deep breath . . . slowly. That's it. More deep breaths . . . relax and close your eyes for a minute . . . I'll be right back . . .'

I followed her into the kitchen. She didn't put on the light. That told me what she was going to do—as if I didn't know already. A pale arrow of light and a chill draught shot across the floor as she silently opened the door of our observation post.

The body was still lying there, outlined in chalk, but otherwise seemingly untouched. Groups of uniforms were working in clusters around the room, paying no further attention to the deceased. One voice rose above the murmur of the others, the words indistinguishable, but followed by a burst of rough laughter.

'Oh!' Evangeline reared back. The sound was jarring and so unseemly. 'That's obscene!'

'They have to laugh to let off steam. Also it's a way of distancing themselves.' My life as a comedienne had taught me the many strange ways of laughter. 'They couldn't stand the job if they had to take every death personally.'

'Just the same . . .' Evangeline still found it unsatisfactory. Maybe it was, but it kept people sane.

'WHAT THE HELL ARE YOU UP TO NOW?' Jasper suddenly bounded across the room and slammed the door shut.

'Now you've done it,' Evangeline said bitterly, as the *bang* reverberated through the kitchen and, doubtless, through the yawning chasm outside.

'Are you trying to kill yourselves?' Jasper was still in a filthy temper. 'That's dangerous! How did you get that door open? It's supposed to be kept locked.'

'Well, it wasn't,' I said. 'It's been unlocked ever since we moved in. And we *did* nearly fall out of it. That's why we keep that chair in front of it . . . usually.'

'Oh God,' Jasper groaned. 'Where's the key?' He glared at the keyhole as though the key might suddenly materialize in it.

'If it's that dangerous,' Evangeline said, 'you ought to have it bricked up.'

'*If? If?*' Jasper looked at her incredulously. 'You mean there's some doubt about it? You think you might be able to step outside there and fly down to earth? Well, perhaps *you* could.'

'There's no need to be rude,' Evangeline said coldly.

'Why don't we go back into the drawing-room and have another drink?' I had the feeling that we should be as far away from that door as possible when the police arrived.

Maybe we could deny we even knew it existed? Claim that it must have been one of the other doors abutting on the empty space that had slammed? It was worth a try.

'Good thinking.' Evangeline saw the merit of the idea. She swooped for the drawing-room. We were distributed around it, sipping our brandy and looking relaxed and innocent when the doorbell rang.

'Jasper, dear, would you—' The steel beneath the velvet of Evangeline's tone sent Jasper stumbling to answer the door. I worry about that boy—he doesn't seem to have enough resilience to the little vicissitudes of life.

Inspector Crichton seemed younger than ever as he stormed into the drawing-room with two uniformed police officers towering over him. Although he looked almost childlike, he was not a child I would like to see having a temper tantrum and I suspected he was perilously close to one.

He walked past us without a word and went straight into the kitchen. We heard the door open, then a long silence until it slammed shut again. When he returned, his mood had not improved.

'Now, ladies.' He gave us a glacial look. 'I should be most interested in any statements you care to make.'

I couldn't think of a word to say. It occurred to me that the Inspector might be seriously considering the possibility that poor Eric had plunged to his death from *our* kitchen door and I was dumbstruck. If only Evangeline had been.

'It's about time!' Unfortunately, she was only too vocal. 'I don't know what your superiors would say if they knew it took you so long to talk to us. However—' She forgave him graciously. 'You're here now, so sit down and let's put our heads together and pool our information. Tell me: what time did the murder take place?'

There was a thundering silence. I saw one of the policemen quietly slip a notebook out of his pocket and prepare to take notes. The peculiar glint in his eye made me suspect that he was less interested in recording possible evidence than in not missing a word of the Inspector's explosion for recounting to his colleagues later.

'Has anyone told you about our prowler?' I asked quickly.

'Oh, we have a prowler now, have we?' Inspector Crichton rounded on me and I wished I'd remained silent. 'Are you sure we haven't had a jewel robbery, as well?'

'We have no need of publicity stunts, Inspector.' Evangeline froze him with a glance—or tried to. Inspector Crichton did not freeze easily. 'We are trying to be helpful.'

'Naturally, naturally.' Inspector Crichton's smile might have been reassuring, had it been less sardonic. 'It cheers our hearts, the way the public is always so eager to help the police with their inquiries.'

'There *is* a prowler,' I insisted. 'Ask anyone. The other residents warned us about him. They think he's one of the locals. They've had a lot of trouble with the locals. Their cars have been damaged so badly they've had to go into the garage for repairs—and now they're afraid the violence is going to escalate. If the prowler lurking outside should get into the building—and maybe he has—'

'And poor dear Eric caught him prowling about The Chummery—' Evangeline took up the scenario with a bit too much zest. 'Eric confronted him . . . challenged him . . . tried to throw him out . . . threatened to call the police . . . there was a struggle . . .'

'The prowler yanked open the door to escape,' I chimed in. 'Not realizing it was the wrong door . . . the one that opened on to empty space. He reeled back . . . Eric advanced on him and they grappled . . . getting closer and closer to the edge of the cliff—I mean, to where the door was still open—'

'The chasm yawning below!' Evangeline was not going

to be left out. 'Their struggle carries them closer . . . they're swaying on the threshold . . . Eric fights like a lion, but he's weakening . . . no match for the brute force of the ruffian . . .'

'They sway back into the room . . . then out towards the abyss again . . .' I could almost see it happening.

'Back and forth . . . back and forth . . . until—' Evangeline swept her hand out and down. 'Over! Perhaps one last despairing cry . . .' She frowned judiciously. 'Perhaps not . . . just the thud as Eric's body hits the floor so far below . . . and the ruffian slinks away . . .'

We looked at each other and nodded, well pleased with our reconstruction of the crime.

There was a strange sound in the room. Evangeline's eyes widened and I'm sure mine did, too, as we realized the enormity of the insult.

We were being given the slow handclap. By that snotty kid Inspector.

'Well, it *could* have happened that way,' I said defensively.

'No, it couldn't!' Whose side was Jasper on? We both glared at him. 'Those doors opening on to the unfinished part of the building are kept locked.'

'*Ours* wasn't,' Evangeline reminded him.

I cleared my throat. Inspector Crichton was listening with entirely too much interest. I cleared my throat again, louder this time.

Evangeline and Jasper stopped bickering abruptly. Inspector Crichton shot me a poisonous glance. I looked at him innocently and looked away. There was a long silence.

The doorbell rang. Inspector Crichton gestured to us to stay where we were and gestured to one of his team to answer it.

'You are all right?' Lazlo Tronnix bounced into the drawing-room, stopping short with a sigh of relief when he saw us sitting there. 'You are all safe? Then why are the police here? The fire-engines I have seen out front before, but never the police cars. Which one have they come to arrest?'

'No one,' Jasper said quickly. 'There's been an accident, a terrible accident. Eric's dead.'

'Eric?' Lazlo looked blank.

'From The Chummery,' Jasper said. 'One of the quiet ones.'

'The Chummery,' Lazlo repeated thoughtfully. 'Not a good situation for the modern world. No.' He shook his head. 'In India, in the days of the Raj, when they were all in the army together, it was one thing. But, in the modern world . . .' He shook his head again.

'Pardon me, sir.' Inspector Crichton was looking a bit confused. 'Are you saying the residents of The Chummery are veterans of the Raj?'

'Only in spirit,' Lazlo said. 'Only in spirit.'

'What about fact?' Inspector Crichton was getting irritable again. 'Who are you and where do you fit in here?'

'I am Lazlo Tronnix. I have the penthouse across the hall. I am a neighbour and, I hope—' he smiled at us— 'a friend.'

'I see.' Inspector Crichton did not look pleased with what he saw. 'And how long have you lived here, sir?'

'Off and on, since the building was restored. It is quite convenient for my City offices and I keep it as a *pied-à-terre* in this country.'

'What, precisely, does off and on mean, sir?'

'Do you know all the residents, Lazlo?' Evangeline butted in. 'What do you think of them.'

'Dear lady—' Naturally, Lazlo answered Evangeline first, or started to.

'Just one moment, sir.' Inspector Crichton glared at Lazlo and Evangeline impartially. 'We'll speak to each of you privately, if you don't mind.'

'Really!' Evangeline *did* mind. Her eyes widened, her nostrils flared, her back arched and she began hyperventilating.

If Inspector Crichton had had any sensitivity at all—or if he had read the script—he would have tugged his forelock, said, 'Beg pardon, Ma'am,' and slunk away. As it was, he stood there watching her sardonically, one eyebrow tilted assessingly. I was afraid he was going to break into that slow handclap again.

'If you're *quite* finished, madam,' he said instead.

'Be careful, young man.' Lazlo's frown hinted at powerful friends, strings that could be pulled, beats that a foolish young copper could find himself back walking. He exuded subtle menace. 'Be very careful.'

'I'm always careful, sir,' Inspector Crichton said. He surveyed each one of us thoughtfully and unerringly settled on the weakest link.

'If we could start with you, sir,' he said to Jasper.

'Divide and conquer,' I remarked bitterly as all the action swung across the hall to Jasper's penthouse. 'In our day, the police never minded about questioning everybody all together in a group. They got clues from watching other suspects' reactions to the one answering the questions.'

'I think,' Lazlo said delicately, 'that perhaps that only happened in films. It made for many dramatic and satisfying moments, but perhaps the results would not always stand up in court. In any case, many rules have changed since then. We must leave it to the good Inspector to conduct his inquiries in the way he sees fit.'

'But he's doing it all wrong,' Evangeline complained. 'Why is he questioning poor Jasper instead of going out looking for that prowler? Find him and you've found the killer.'

'There has been a prowler?' Lazlo's interest sharpened. 'In this building?'

'Well, outside,' Evangeline said, 'waiting his chance to get in. We've been warned not to let any strangers into the building because of that. I've seen him lurking about myself. Nasty, suspicious-looking man, pretending to be waiting for someone on the street corner. Just the sort of person who'd ruin expensive cars and try to get into the building to do more damage.'

I decided not to remind her that she'd originally thought he was a plainclothes policeman. He was now her one and only nomination for culprit, despite the fact that all the residents were on their guard against him and it was highly unlikely that he had ever got into the building.

'But I do not understand.' Lazlo had a puzzled frown. 'How can you be so certain that it was murder and not an accident? Jasper says it was an accident.'

'Experience.' Evangeline gave him a pitying smile. 'Dear Jasper does not have my wealth of experience. When I worked in *The Happy Couple* series, it was *never* an accident.'

CHAPTER 15

By next day, it seemed that Evangeline had been correct.

A brisk and efficient team of policemen we hadn't seen before marched into our flat and officially sealed our dangerous kitchen door. We heard later that they had done the same in all the flats with doors opening on to the open space. That didn't make it any the more acceptable to Evangeline.

'The unmitigated gall!' she raged. 'And the idiocy! Locking the stable door after the horse has been stolen. What do they hope to accomplish by sealing that door now?'

'Privacy, maybe?' I suggested. 'Jasper really blew it when he slammed that door. Now they know all those doors are prime eavesdropping posts—and they're still working down on the floor.'

'You couldn't hear much of anything from our door,' Evangeline said fretfully. 'We're too far up.'

'We could hear the voices on the stairs,' I reminded her.

'That's right. We need to know what they were up to. All that shouting and threatening—'

'Do you think we should tell the police? It might mean someone had a motive for murdering Eric.' The more I thought about it, the better the idea seemed.

'The police are not being cooperative,' Evangeline pronounced sternly. 'They don't deserve to be told anything.'

'The police aren't supposed to be cooperative with us,' I pointed out. 'We're suspects.'

'Do you think so?' She was almost mollified. 'No. No, we're not. If we are, they'd have questioned us properly instead of assuming we'd know nothing about the murder just because we were out of the building when it happened.'

'We don't. And we weren't here. And we ought to tell Inspector Crichton everything we know, because he'll be getting information from a lot of other sources and he can put everything together. Not that we can tell him much. We didn't even know Eric. He was just one of the non-speaking extras helping the others move in the furniture—' I paused, something flickering uneasily at the edge of my consciousness. 'Although maybe we shouldn't mention anything about *that* to Inspector Crichton.'

'You see.' Evangeline smiled smugly. 'You don't trust him to come up with the right answers, either.'

'It's not that. Not exactly. It's just—' I gave up. I couldn't put it into words, not even to myself.

'And we shouldn't say anything about Mariah to the police.'

'Mariah?' She'd startled me.

'There must be a good reason why everyone in the building is so afraid of her. She *seems* all right—but they *know* her. Her dark secrets . . . her hidden depths . . . her *madness* . . .'

'Oh, now wait a minute—'

'Think about it, Trixie.'

'*You* think about it. Jasper said all these people were friends before they moved in here. If they knew anything like that about Mariah, why would they have let her in, in the first place?'

'Perhaps it wasn't so noticeable on a casual working or even friendship basis. She could seem all right during daylight hours or even part of the night. But on a constant seven-day-a-week basis . . . or perhaps just when the moon was full . . .'

'I give up, Evangeline! I give up on you completely! Jasper is right. You've acted on too many B pictures and crazy El Cheapos. You'd better not go around saying anything like that to the police—or you're the one who'll wind up in a loony-bin.'

'All right.' Evangeline folded her arms and faced me. 'So what's your explanation for the way they treat Mariah?'

'I don't have an explanation, but when I come up with one, it won't be one that will get me sued for slander.'

'It was the loony-bin a minute ago.'

'Probably both.' But she was right. We still didn't know why everyone hated Mariah so. 'Anyway, if there was something of that sort wrong with Mariah, surely Eric would never have let her get within pushing distance of him.'

'And then there's Sophie,' Evangeline said reflectively.

'Sophie? How did she get into this? Everybody likes Sophie.'

'Perhaps, but does Sophie like them? We mustn't forget there was an earlier murder. Sophie's sister. Sophie may have had reason to believe that Eric had something to do with that and impulsively tried to revenge her—and then regretted it. She's the only one around here I'd bet on to show any remorse. People with tempers are usually very good at remorse. They have to be, they hurt so many feelings.'

'Because of the crying we heard?' I considered the idea. 'That could have been either a man or a woman. Besides, Frederick seems to be with her all the time. She couldn't get away long enough to kill anyone—unless he was in it with her.'

'That, too, is possible.' Evangeline nodded judiciously.

'It's a lot more possible that Sandra died because of a mugging that went wrong,' I said. 'Or maybe not even a mugging. Maybe the prowler wanted to teach one of the Yuppies a lesson—and went too far. He may have just meant to beat her up, but he hit too hard and killed her instead. Then he shoved her into the river, hoping the body would be carried out to sea.'

'And the murderer always returns to the scene of the crime!' Evangeline said enthusiastically. 'Trixie, I think you've hit it! That's why he's still lurking about, trying to find out what's happening and whether anyone suspects him. And perhaps Eric was a witness and had only just remembered something—and that was why Eric had to be killed, too.'

'I'm not so sure about that—'

'Furthermore, I don't believe Jasper has told us all he knows.' Her tone did not bode well for Jasper. 'Far from it.'

'Jasper seems to have an awful lot on his mind.' I tried to defend him.

'And more by the minute. I wouldn't like to be in his shoes when Juanita and Beau get back from their world cruise.'

'Yeah, Beau is going to be in a filthy mood after spending all that money.' I couldn't help grinning.

'And he needn't think Juanita's going to let him off the hook for just one little world cruise.' Evangeline grinned back. 'She's going to make him spend money like a drunken sailor from now on. He owes it to her.'

'Owes . . .' The word tugged at my consciousness. Money . . . the lack of it . . . the problems with it . . . the people who had it . . . the people who wanted it. Money. The preoccupation with money throbbed through this building like a themesong through a major musical.

'Jasper owes a lot of money. Nigel claims Sophie and Frederick owed money to Sandra. They're borrowing from Lazlo, too . . .'

'That's right,' Evangeline said. 'It would have made a lot more sense if it had been Lazlo who was murdered.'

'Somebody already tried to send his companies crashing.'

'Oh, come along, Trixie. You know and I know that it was Nigel starting that rumour.'

'Was it? He said he heard it from somebody else.'

'Nonsense! If it wasn't Nigel, I'll eat the entire wardrobe of Hedda Hopper's hats!'

'Gosh, I haven't thought of her in years. But I'm afraid you're right. I can't imagine who else it could be but Nigel. He was so . . . so sneaky about it.'

'It's his nature. I wonder what Sandra saw in him.'

'Maybe they were soulmates. Just because she was Sophie's sister doesn't mean they were at all alike.'

'No.' Evangeline pursed her lips judiciously, considering this. 'They couldn't have been—or Sophie wouldn't have needed money.'

'Not unless Frederick turned out to be a lot more expensive than she'd bargained for.' We'd seen a lot of that in Hollywood, although the most expensive gents had usually had titles to offer—and wonderful stories about how only the peasants on their estates had ever worked. The least diplomatic told these stories so often that even the dumbest glamour girl finally figured out just who it was who was supposed to be the peasant in this *ménage*. That was when the Prince, the Count, the Baron or the Lord found themselves and their valet and their monogrammed luggage standing on the sidewalk with a one-way ticket back to the Old Country. Only it usually worked out that they stayed in Hollywood and found themselves another female meal ticket.

'I wonder if Sophie and Frederick *really* get along as well as they seem to—or whether the marriage might be fraying a bit around the edges?'

Evangeline sure ought to be an expert on that situation. I nodded, keeping my mouth shut, for once. She took it as encouragement.

'When you think of the way they're always together . . . He never seems to leave her alone for a minute. You might think he was more of a jailer than a husband.'

'Are you suggesting she's crazy, too? How about a male nurse?' Insanity seemed to have become Evangeline's favourite motive. But . . . 'Now that you mention it, I've never seen them apart. Of course, we haven't lived here all that long.'

'Long enough,' Evangeline sighed. 'It's beginning to feel like a lifetime.'

'That's because it's so hard to get away from here. If we were closer to the West End, or still in St John's Wood, there'd be so much to do we'd be busy every minute.'

'St John's Wood.' Evangeline sighed again, nostalgically this time. 'I dreamt about dear St John's Wood last night. And Swiss Cottage. Do you know where I'd really like to live? In that lovely block of flats right over the supermarket in Swiss Cottage. We'd just have to go out the door and everything would be spread in front of us: the shops, the restaurants, the cinema, the buses to the West End . . .'

'How right you are! That would be an ideal place to live.'
A sudden wild hope rose in me. 'Why don't we get over
there and see about it? We can call a taxi—'

'We can't do anything until the end of the quarter.' Evangeline squelched me firmly. 'Besides,' she switched to a
coaxing tone, 'you wouldn't want to leave here just when
things are getting so interesting, would you?'

'Wouldn't I?'

'The police won't allow us to leave until their investigations are complete.'

'The police don't give a damn about us. Sandra was
killed before we moved in and we have solid alibis for the
entire day that Eric was murdered.' She didn't want to face
the fact that we were out of this one; it was far more interesting to be a suspect . . . or a sleuth.

'Look—' I tried again. 'Why don't we go to Town? We
can forget about all this and make a day of it. We can go
shopping, have an early dinner and catch a show.'

'At a time like this? When our friends need us? When
Jasper needs us?'

Uh-oh, I could see it coming. She was going to take an
active part in the investigation—or start one of her own.

'No, Trixie.' She got a far-away look in her eyes, a noble
resignation straightened her shoulders. 'We cannot desert
our posts.'

'We're not in the Foreign Legion.'

'We still have our duty.' The pose was straight out of
Dedication, as the nurse watched the last troopship pull out
from the dock, leaving her and the mortally-wounded sol-
diers on the shore, and knew that she had to continue nurs-
ing them until the last one had died—or until the enemy
swept out of the jungle to slaughter them all.

'What we *will* do—' Evangeline became brisk and
businesslike—'is go down and call on Sophie and

Frederick. We'll see how they're coping and make our reservations for Sunday lunch. If they're still planning to carry on with it.'

There was almost a party going on in the communal sitting-room at the end of the corridor on the restaurant floor. Evangeline was quite put out for a moment because we hadn't been invited, but the group greeted us so warmly that it soon became evident that the party was one of those gatherings that had just grown.

'I came down to get a book to read,' Hamish said. (Where had we heard that line before?) 'And I found old Nigel here, so we started to talk, then Roz happened along. Frederick and Sophie heard us talking and came out to join us. Everything just snowballed from there. I went back to The Chummery to get a bottle and Sebastian and George came back with me—it's pretty bleak up there right now. Sophie nipped into the kitchen and whipped up these cheese-and-sesame straws. Do have one—' He offered the plate to me.

'Delicious!' I took another one. Evangeline abstractedly helped herself to several and sat down.

'Plenty more.' Sophie was almost cheerful for the first time since we'd met her. 'I'll just pop another batch in the oven.' She hurried off.

'Why don't I go and bring down a bottle or two for our contribution?' I started for the lift.

'Not necessary,' Hamish said. 'You must let us repay your hospitality.' But the level in their bottle was so low that it wouldn't have been much of a repayment.

'I'll be right back,' I said over my shoulder.

I should have looked where I was going. I cannoned into Lazlo, who was already in the lift.

'Sorry,' I gasped, 'but you might as well get out here. This is where all the action is tonight. I'm just going to get another bottle and it looks like we're settling down for the evening.'

'I shall accompany you, if I may.' Although he wasn't wearing a hat, he gave the impression of raising one to me. 'And then I shall join the party as your escort.'

'That's fine with me.' The lift was ascending again. 'Maybe we ought to knock on Jasper's door and see if he's around. He could use some cheering up, too.'

'Yes, it has not been a salubrious time for the residents of this unhappy building. We must hope that the dark clouds have now rolled safely past.' He didn't sound as though he believed it for a minute.

'Mmmm.' Neither did I. 'I think the police are going to have to strut their stuff and cart somebody away before the rest of us can relax again. And maybe not even then. Unless—' I brightened. 'Unless it really was the prowler doing the murders.'

'Oh, yes, that prowler.' Lazlo frowned as the door slid open at our floor.

'What I do not understand—' he was still frowning as he followed me into the penthouse—'is why did they not simply notify the police to take care of this man?'

'Who knows?' Since he was going to help me carry everything, I added a few frozen pizzas to the bottles; Sophie could cook them, her oven was already warmed up. 'I don't get the impression that they're very keen on the police around here.'

Jasper wasn't home yet, so I slipped a note under his door. Although, if he heard all the noise from the impromptu party, curiosity would compel him to investigate before he reached his flat.

There is a euphoria that sets in at a certain stage if the party is going well. This time it seemed to arrive at the same instant Lazlo and I stepped out of the lift with the additional refreshments.

A ragged cheer went up. Nigel dashed forward to rescue the bottles that were beginning to slip from my grasp.

'Oh, bless you!' Sophie swooped on the frozen pizzas. 'I honestly didn't feel like doing any more cooking.'

'Great idea, great idea.' Frederick helped her carry them out into the kitchen.

There was a babble of voices from the head of the stairs leading up from the main lobby. Several more young people appeared; I recognized most of them from last Sunday's lunch on *The Gliding Gourmet.*

'Come on!' Roz waved to her flatmates. 'Join the party!' She turned to me, flushed and happy. 'This is the way we thought it was going to be when we moved in. Lots of social life and impromptu parties. Instead—' Her face shadowed.

'Here you are.' Nigel thrust a drink into my hands. It was about time. 'Your very good health!'

'And yours.' I returned the toast, a pleasant glow spreading through me—and not just because of the drink. I'd only had a sip. It was the sudden burgeoning of camaraderie, laughter and mutual approval. This was what Jasper had obviously been aiming for: The Chummery, on a larger scale.

The noise level rose; everyone talking to everyone else and laughing. Everyone friends and partners in a safe refuge where they could rest united against the hostile world.

This was the way it had been meant to be. Why, then— and how—had it gone so very wrong?

There was an abrupt silence; more than a silence, a vacuum, as though all the air and life had been drawn out of the upper lobby. Everyone had turned and was staring at me. No, beyond me. I turned slowly to see what they were staring at.

The other lift had stopped and disgorged its passengers: Mariah. Mariah again. But Jasper was with her. And, stepping from behind them both: Inspector Crichton.

'Well, well, well. His bright childlike gaze swept the scene, but there was nothing childlike about the insinuation in his eyes and tone. Had he been taking lessons in nastiness from Superintendent Heyhoe? Or did all policemen reach the same level of suspicion and distaste independently?

'Having a celebration, are we? I wonder why?'

CHAPTER 16

'There's nothing else for it.' Evangeline announced what she had intended to do all along. 'I shall have to take this investigation into my own hands.'

'No, please, Evangeline.' I made a vain attempt to head her off. 'Why don't you just go on Lazlo's Board of Directors instead?'

She snorted and poured herself another cup of coffee.

I'd hoped she might have cooled down overnight, but no such luck. Her dander was well and truly up and she wanted to teach Inspector Crichton a lesson.

'I'll Admirable *him!*' Evangeline lifted her head and stared into middle-distance with firm resolution. 'Trixie, we are going to teach that young whippersnapper the lesson of his life!'

'Include me out.' I began backing towards my room. 'I'm sure you can manage that fine all by yourself.'

'Naturally, I can, but—' Evangeline gave me an injured look. 'I wouldn't want to leave you out of all the fun. You know you'd be upset if I did.'

'I could live with it.' I almost reached my door.

'Nonsense! Now come and sit down and we'll make out a list.'

'What kind of list?'

'Of the Suspects, of course.' She produced a notebook

and ballpoint pen with a flourish—and waited for the applause.

'Uh-huh.' Unfortunately, I was fresh out of applause.

'And just who do you have in mind?'

'We must be completely impartial. So we'll start with Jasper and Lazlo. We didn't see them all day.'

'Oh, now, wait a minute. We don't even know when it happened. Eric could have been lying there for hours. Or, like Sandra, for days.'

'Not days.' She frowned at me. 'He helped with moving the furniture that morning and, now that I come to think about it, he wasn't very happy about doing it.'

'I noticed that. Maybe Hamish twisted his arm to loan us something he didn't want to part with—even temporarily.'

'Trixie, that's a brilliant observation.' Evangeline leaped up and prowled into the drawing-room. 'If only we knew which of the items belonged to him, we might find we have an important clue on our hands.'

'If only,' I echoed, somewhat cynically. 'How do you think we could find out?'

'Mariah!' Evangeline spoke with sudden inspiration. 'I'm sure Mariah must know. You saw her face when she was looking around at everything.'

'Yeah, but remember—' A different echo came back to me. 'Mariah is prepared to swear she didn't see a thing.'

'Jasper, then. I'm sure Jasper knows.'

'Yeah, and *I'm* sure Jasper isn't going to tell.'

'There must be some way of finding out.' Evangeline glared around the room in frustrated bafflement. 'There must!'

'Mmmm, maybe there is.' A vague idea came to me. 'Why don't we ring up and see if Roz is around? We might invite her to join us for coffee.'

*

'Would you like to go over to the supermarket again?' Roz, like Mariah, seemed unsure of a welcome in her own right. 'I was thinking I might do some shopping later, when the crowds have thinned out. I'd be happy to take you along.'

'Oh, I think we have enough for the time being,' Evangeline said grandly.

'Sure,' I said, in the same instant. I have the feeling that you should never pass up the chance for a trip to a supermarket. Like taking every opportunity to avail yourself of a visit to a ladies' room, on the theory that you don't know when the next chance will present itself.

'Er, that's fine, then.' Roz looked from Evangeline to me with a certain bemusement. 'I thought of leaving in about an hour—if that's all right with you.'

'Fine with me.' I got in quickly before Evangeline could start in on the real purpose of the meeting.

A strange buzzer sounded abruptly and Evangeline and I both jumped. It was not the normal friendly peal of the door-bell we had grown accustomed to. Instinctively, we both looked towards the kitchen, where all the high-tech equipment kept leading weird and sinister lives of their own.

'It's for the main entrance downstairs,' Roz identified. 'Are you expecting anyone? You'll have to buzz them in.'

'*I'm* not.' Evangeline looked at me accusingly. 'Who have you invited now?'

'No one.' I crossed and activated the TV monitor for the downstairs entrance. 'Who's there?' I shouted into the intercom.

'Delivery.' A bunch of flowers filled the screen, obscuring the man lurking behind it.

There was something funny here. I paused with my finger hovering over the lock-release button. All those delivery boys had managed to come straight through last week without needing to be let in by us. Why was this man—?

'Don't let him in!' Roz shrieked. She had lost colour and

lurched to her feet. 'It's not a delivery. He's trying to sneak in!'

'It's the Prowler!' Evangeline whooped. 'Come on, Trixie!' She swept past me, grabbing my arm and pulling me along with her. 'We've got him!'

We hadn't, of course. By the time we got downstairs, he had disappeared, only a few fallen petals giving mute witness that anyone had ever been standing there at all.

'Damn!' Evangeline raged, back in the penthouse. 'Damn, damn, damn! We nearly had him.'

'Frankly, I don't give a damn,' I said. 'What would we have done with him if we *had* caught him?'

'We'd get the truth out of him.' Evangeline was an avenging fury. 'One way or another.'

'What truth?' It was just as well he had disappeared. Some sixth sense must have warned him.

'He's getting more brazen about it,' I realized. 'Why should he actually ring our bell if he wants to get in to do damage. He must know we'd seen him on the security screen.'

'If you call that seeing,' Evangeline sniffed. 'He held those miserable wilted flowers so that they hid his face.'

'And he's very fast on his feet.'

'He knew something was up as soon as we didn't buzz him in, so he made his getaway in case we'd called the police. He'll undoubtedly try again—and probably through us. He thinks we don't know what's going on, so he perceives us as the weakest link.'

'Maybe we *don't* know what's going on.' The whole episode was still bothering me. 'There's something awfully funny about this.'

'Funny, indeed,' Evangeline agreed. 'I haven't seen goings on like this since the days of the King's Proctor.'

'Who?'

'He functioned in the days when divorces were hard to

get—and he made it a lot harder. If the parties involved
in the divorce case were discovered to be misbehaving with
other parties and reported to him, he could stop the divorce
proceedings, thus forcing them to remain married.'

'Even if both parties wanted out?'

'That made no difference; they had to behave themselves
to get free. After the initial trip to the hotel room with a
hired third party—a gentleman never involved the true
object of his affections—and once the private detective and
photographer had burst in and taken compromising photo-
graphs, the divorce suit could be filed, the rented co-
respondent paid off, and everyone got on with their own
lives, trying to exercise due discretion.'

'You mean trying not to get caught. It sounds awful.'

'It was, but it was quite exciting, too.' She sighed nostalgically. 'The clandestine meetings, the trysts in small
country hotels, the jumping at shadows and always wondering whether the fellow pausing to light his cigarette under
the streetlamp was as innocent as he seemed. But the laws
changed long ago and I've seen nothing like it these days
until . . .'

'I see what you mean, but that can't be the explanation
here. You said yourself those laws have changed.'

'Apart from which—' she snapped back into the present.
'No one in this building seems to have the time, energy or
inclination to do that sort of fooling around. Young people
these days have no stamina.'

'By the way—' That reminded me. 'Where has Roz
gone?'

'Roz . . . ?' Evangeline looked around vaguely. 'Didn't
she come downstairs with us?'

'Yes, but she disappeared as soon as she saw the Prowler
had gone. Maybe she went to call the police.'

'I wouldn't bet on it, Trixie. The police don't seem to

be too popular around here, and with good reason, I would say.'

Our doorbell—the inner bell—rang abruptly. We looked at each other in consternation.

'He couldn't—' I began.

Evangeline stalked past me and activated the monitor screen. Roz's anxious face sprang into view.

'We were just wondering where you'd gone,' I said, opening the door.

'I—I just thought of something.' She was panting slightly. She bent and struggled with a pedestalled object that wasn't quite a table; below the top was a latticed wood basket lined with faded satin. She managed to pick it up and struggled past me with it.

'*What* is *that?*' Evangeline looked at it as though it might explode.

'It's a Victorian sewing table,' Roz said. 'I thought Trixie might like it for her bedroom.'

'A sewing table? For *Trixie?*' Evangeline hooted with laughter.

'I don't do much sewing,' I explained with simple dignity.

'If she can't cobble it together with safety pins, she throws it away.' Evangeline spoiled the effect I was striving for.

'Oh, I don't expect you to *use* it.' Roz looked horrified at the notion. 'I just thought it would look nice—and fill some of that empty space.' She headed firmly for my bedroom with it.

'Well, thank you,' I said weakly, since she seemed determined that I have it. 'That's very sweet of you.'

'The satin lining of that latticework is all frayed,' Evangeline sniffed. Mind you, if the table had been offered to her, she would have been a lot nicer about it.

'That doesn't matter,' I muttered, thankful that Roz was

safely inside my room and couldn't hear us. 'I'm not going to use it.'

'Good thing! It looks as though it would fall apart if you tried.'

'Shhh!' Roz was re-entering the drawing-room. She looked as though a heavy burden had been lifted from her mind, as well as her hands.

'There,' she beamed. 'I've put a vase of flowers on it and it looks just right—as though it belonged there and had always been there.'

'How lovely!' It was getting a little hard to exude the proper rapture over largesse I had neither requested nor wanted. 'Umm, are we going to the supermarket now?'

'Oh!' She looked stricken. 'I forgot! I, uh, had a telephone call while I was getting the sewing table. I have to go back to the office. Perhaps we could go to the supermarket tomorrow. I'm terribly sorry.' She was already moving towards the front door. 'But it's dreadfully urgent.'

'Tomorrow will be fine,' I assured her, not believing a word of her apology. 'Maybe you could telephone me—'

'Oh, yes. Yes, I'll do that. And thank you for being so understanding.' The door closed behind her.

'Now,' Evangeline raised an eyebrow at me. 'What was that all about?'

'Darned if I know.' I met her gaze with equal suspicion. 'Do you get the feeling there's something going on around here? And I don't just mean murder.'

'There is, and we're going to get to the bottom of it.' Evangeline strode purposefully into my bedroom. 'I want a closer look at that sewing table.'

'So do I.' I was right behind her.

The Victorian sewing table was a delightful object, but Evangeline was impervious to its charms. She eyed it coldly as she circled it, then swooped and snatched the vase of flowers from its inlaid top.

'Hold this!' She thrust the vase at me, one hand already prying at the table lid.

'Do you think we ought—?'

'I'm sure I heard something rattling inside when Roz was dragging it along.' She gave the table an impatient push and it tilted, obligingly demonstrating its rattle again.

'There'll be scissors inside,' I said. 'And spools of thread, an embroidery hoop, maybe a chatelaine. All sorts of period stuff, I expect.'

'Your expectations should be greater.' Evangeline gave me a pitying look as she raised the lid and lifted out a swatch of dotted Swiss muslin which she unrolled to disclose a jewellery box. 'It was a good ploy, putting a vase of flowers on top. Most people wouldn't have disturbed it, at least not until the flowers died.'

'Oh!' I nearly dropped the vase; I set it down hastily on the bedside table. 'Do you think Roz realizes she left that in there?'

'Don't be naïve, Trixie. That was obviously the purpose of this whole charade. Now why would she want to plant this stuff on us?'

'Maybe she doesn't want it in her own apartment,' I suggested. 'Not with the police climbing around all over the building.'

'Do you think it's hot?' Evangeline's eyes gleamed.

'That's possible, I suppose, but I find it hard to picture Roz as a jewel thief.'

'I wouldn't put *anything* past anyone in this place!'

The feeling would have been mutual if they could have seen Evangeline sliding her fingernail into the little crack between the fragile lid and the box.

'Don't *do* that—you'll break it!'

'You're right.' She withdrew her fingernail and examined it critically. 'There's probably a key somewhere.' She began delving into the tiny pink satin pockets lining the inside rim of the sewing table. They disgorged embroidery scissors, flower-painted china buttons, packets of needles and pins in their original printed paper wrappers and, finally, a miniature key.

'I still don't think you ought to do it,' I protested feebly as she fitted it into the lock.

'You're hampered by an over-developed sense of privacy.' Evangeline turned the key and threw back the lid. 'You'll never learn anything that way.'

I drew closer as she began lifting out the pieces one by one. Each was an exquisite example of the best of modern jewellery. Smooth sweeps of solid gold studded with chunky glittering stones, some pieces signed with famous designer names.

'These cost a pretty penny,' Evangeline said. 'There's not a carat below fourteen here—and most are eighteen or twenty-two. The gems are first quality, too.'

'And they're Roz.' I could see her wearing them and handing them down with pride to future generations.

'They're definitely Roz. You can forget any jewel thief nonsense—these pieces could have been made for her.'

'Perhaps they were.' Evangeline tried a square-cut emerald framed in a gleaming satin-finish gold against her own ear lobe and sighed enviously.

'Put it down, Evangeline.' It was time to be firm with her. 'You know you could never get away with it.'

'They're for pierced ears, anyway.' Reluctantly, Evangeline replaced the earring. Roz could thank her lucky stars that extreme physical cowardice had kept Evangeline from ever having had her ears pierced.

'So much for that theory.' I brought her briskly back to order. 'What next?'

'Lazlo?' Evangeline murmured thoughtfully. 'He seems to have jewels to throw around, too. Do you think he gave these to her . . . for services rendered, perhaps?'

'Considering the jewels he threw at us, that's ingratitude for you!'

'Too many people have been throwing their treasure at us, Trixie. It's becoming quite noticeable. Suspicious, even.'

I hesitated to call her an ingrate again because she had a point there. One or two favours were only to be expected, but the veritable cascade of offerings showered upon us was enough to give one pause. I discovered I didn't really believe that *quid pro quo* story about Desert Island Discs, either.

'Let's face it, Trixie.' Evangeline put everything back into the jewellery box, locked it and swathed it again in its dotted Swiss muslin shroud. 'We've been had.'

She closed the top of the sewing table, stopping just short of slamming it down and replaced the vase of flowers, then stood back, staring at it and brooding.

'I can feel it in my bones, Trixie. I'm not sure how and I don't know why—but we've been had!'

CHAPTER 17

Evangeline went back to her list of suspects with renewed vigour, but cabin fever was setting in so far as I was concerned. Especially since the prospect of a trip to the supermarket had been dangled in front of me and then whisked away.

Abruptly, I was determined to have it just the same— and today, not tomorrow. I rootled through my handbag and found Eddie's card.

'The neighbourhood's gone down since all them Yuppies moved in.' Eddie expertly spun the steering wheel, taking us out of the supermarket parking lot. My shopping bags slid across the cab floor and crashed against the opposite door.

'Ruined everything, they have.' He swung the wheel in the other direction and the bags slid back the other way. I stuck out my foot to try to stop them, but the seat belt held me immobile and there was nothing more I could do. I realized that Eddie was just expressing his resentment, but that didn't make it any easier for me.

'And now they're killing each other,' Eddie said bitterly. 'That doesn't surprise me a bit. Too bad it didn't happen earlier, before they destroyed everything for everyone else.' He ground the gears. 'Never mind, they'll get what's coming to them—and soon now.'

'You won't have anything to do with that, I hope.' I spoke sharply. 'They have quite enough problems now and I think it's pretty rotten of your friends to harass them the way they've been doing.'

'What are you talking about?' He twisted round to stare at me.

'You know very well what I'm talking about. And please watch the road.'

'Now see here—' He pulled over to the kerb and slammed on the brake. 'I thought you were a nice lady. What are you insinuating?'

'I'm insinuating nothing,' I said coldly. (I'd find bruises where I'd been flung against that seat belt.) 'I'm stating a fact. The locals around here have been relieving their feelings of injustice by petty little acts of vandalism. They've been damaging cars belonging to the residents of our building—in some cases, so badly that the cars have had to go into the garage for expensive repairs.'

'Never!' He said it with such outraged vehemence that I found myself believing him. 'Who told you that? It's a bare-faced lie!'

'I suppose,' I said, with growing unease, 'you're going to tell me that none of your friends are lurking around, trying to sneak into the building to do more damage.'

'Of course not! Where did you get such an idea? That's actionable, that is. We ought to sue!'

'OK, Eddie, take it easy. I think I believe you.' And I was beginning to remember just who had planted these ideas in my mind.

'I should hope so! It's God's own truth. The people around here wouldn't dirty their hands going near that lot. We don't need to.' The corners of his mouth quirked in a vulpine leer.

'They'll get theirs. Right where it hurts them most. But it won't be from any of us.'

'What do you mean?'

'Oh, no, you don't.' He started the taxi. 'I'm not telling you anything more. You'll only get the wrong end of the stick again, and I don't want to be responsible.'

I'd hate to think my girlish wiles weren't working any more but, although I exerted them to the utmost, I didn't get another thing out of Eddie.

It didn't matter. I already had enough of a lead to go on with.

'I think I ought to throw a party,' I told Evangeline after a long brooding ascent in the wrong lift. Someone had been using the other one, but I had been so perplexed and annoyed that I had not minded the enforced incarceration—it had given me some quiet time in which to consider the situation.

'Good idea. We'll invite all the suspects. And dear sweet Superintendent Ho-Hum and—'

'Not us.' I reined her in. 'Me. It will be my party. The invitations will be going out under my name.' And that should end certain people's idea that I was some sort of paid companion to Evangeline.

'Well!' she huffed. 'I don't know why you feel that way about it.'

And may she never find out!

'I'll charter *The Gliding Gourmet*, I think.' That would take care of the catering, give Frederick and Sophie something to concern themselves with, and provide a familiar and non-threatening venue for the festivities.

'Yes.' Evangeline had been thinking it over and turning the idea to her own advantage. 'Yes, that will do splendidly. With you as hostess, I shall be free to get on with my investigations. Hey-Day and I will circulate inconspicuously among the guests and learn—'

'It's not Superintendent Heyhoe's case!' I snapped in exasperation. 'Inspector Crichton is in charge.'

'You wouldn't invite *him!*'

'Oh, yes, I would!' I hadn't thought of it before, but now she had me riled. 'Besides, Heyhoe will never come near us again.'

'He won't be able to stay away,' she smirked. 'I know the signs. He may not think he likes us but, in truth, we fascinate him.

'That's what you think! What he'd really like is to pin everything on us—and I mean everything. Not just the murders but everything up to and including the Recession. He's sure that, somehow, everything has to be our fault.'

'Well . . .' She shrugged as though I had just proved her point. 'Isn't that a form of fascination.'

'I'd call it obsession—and I'd call it dangerous.'

'Oh, Trixie!' She shrugged again. 'You simply don't understand. But, I'll guarantee you—if you invite him, he'll come.'

*

I decided to consult Frederick about my idea, fearing that it might be rather tactless to ask Sophie to cater a party at a time like this.

On the other hand, I was fairly sure she could use the money. Even if she was sole heiress, it takes a long time to settle an estate, especially when the lawyers have to wait for the outcome of a police investigation to be certain that they aren't allowing the culprit to profit from his or her crime.

And there was going to be the added complication of Nigel. The way he was going around proclaiming himself Sandra's common-law husband suggested he was working up to contesting the will—if there was one. If there wasn't, he might have an even stronger case under the emerging palimony legislations.

I suddenly wondered if any of the furniture he had contributed to the penthouse was really Sandra's—and if Sophie knew about it.

'A party?' Frederick was enthusiastic the moment I mentioned it. 'Wonderful idea! Everyone could do with some cheering up right now, and Sophie needs something to do. A job she can really get her teeth into. Have you any ideas about the menu? Perhaps a pasta buffet? Lasagne and cannelloni and spaghetti with big bowls of various sauces?'

'I was thinking more of something along the filet mignon line,' I said firmly. I suspected that too many of our little chums had been living on spaghetti and baked beans for too long. They needed a proper meal.

'Tournedos Rossini!' Frederick grew even more enthusiastic. 'Marvellous! Everyone will love that. It will remind them of the good old—' He broke off abruptly.

'With asparagus,' I said, as though I hadn't noticed. 'And potatoes in some form or other.'

'Leave it to us.' He recovered smoothly. 'You want a sit-down meal, then? A dinner party?'

'No . . .' The thought was tempting, but a dinner party

would be too static. I wanted something where the guests could move around more freely. Given the circumstances, no one would want to be stuck sitting next to a policeman all evening.

'No, you can serve that buffet-style, can't you?' I was suddenly anxious, remembering the restricted space of *The Gliding Gourmet*. 'Or would that be too awkward on the boat?'

'It might be, but I have a better idea. We'll inaugurate the Shore Dining Room with your party,' Frederick said grandly. 'At least, part of it. You won't be inviting enough people to fill it completely, will you?'

'Not really. It will be a medium-sized party. Basically, just our regular group and the other residents, plus a few outside friends of mine.' I didn't want to admit the police were going to be among them. 'Er . . . there won't be any difficulty with Sophie about my having Nigel at the party?'

'Oh, no, she's over that now.' He spoke easily, but the look in his eyes didn't quite match the confidence of his tone. 'She was terribly upset with Nigel at the time, but she's calmed down now.'

'Mmm . . .' I accepted the statement without actually believing it. 'Well, I'll trust you to make sure there's no unpleasantness. I wouldn't want my guests subjected to another scene.' Nor did I wish to witness another scene myself, for that matter.

'Of course, of course. Have no fear. I'll see to everything. Now, shall we get down to details?'

After a pleasant hour with Frederick (where was Sophie all this time, I wondered; this was the first time I had seen them apart), everything was settled. Drinks (I vetoed champagne on the grounds that it was too associated with celebrations and might be considered in poor taste) and canapes would be served in the reception area outside the dining-room. The buffet would be set out in the dining-room and small tables would accommodate groups of four and six. If the weather was fine, the party would adjourn to *The Gliding Gourmet* for dessert, coffee and liqueurs. The changes of scene would give everyone the opportunity to mingle and ensure that nobody was stuck with the same people throughout the party, which would be on Sunday. Short notice, perhaps, but Frederick assured me that practically everyone had already made their reservations for that day and would be delighted to discover that someone else was picking up the tab—and for a better meal than they had anticipated.

That left the invitations to be issued. I had already resolved to deliver them in person and the shortness of time made an excellent excuse for the informality.

I still hadn't had a look inside The Chummery. This was the perfect moment to remedy that . . .

I stood for an inordinately long time outside the door. Aware that I was being scrutinized on the monitor inside, I put on my most appealing smile and made hopeful door-opening gestures.

For a long time, nothing happened and I was just beginning to wonder if I was imagining that I was being observed when the door opened a crack.

'What do *you* want?' a voice growled. I'd had warmer welcomes in my time.

'Hamish?' I didn't for a moment think it was, but I felt that uttering a name might provide some sort of credentials. At least, it established that I knew who lived here. I hadn't just knocked on any door.

'He isn't here.' But the door opened a further grudging inch. 'He's out.'

'Sebastian?' I tried again. 'Is that you?'

'Sebastian isn't here, either.' The door opened enough to reveal a glowering George. 'They've both gone out. But not together.'

'Oh, I see.' I saw—and smelled—more than that. George was as royally drunk as any of the legendary topers of the industry. 'Well, do you think I might come in and talk to you?'

'Why?' he demanded, with a truculence worthy of W. C. Fields, then seemed to change his mind. 'Why not?' He threw open the door with a swagger Errol Flynn might have envied and leered at me.

'Come in.' He stepped back and beckoned coyly. I began to wonder if I really wanted to, but it was too late to back down now.

'Always glad to talk to you.' He nodded emphatically at me, closing the door with a decisive click. 'Haven't had much chance to talk recently. Not speaking to Hamish. Sebastian, either. Sent them to Coventry, where they belong. Wish they'd go there and stay there.'

'Oh, but I thought you were all such good friends.' I sidled past him before either of us could change our minds. 'Isn't this The Chummery?'

'That was then, this is now. The Hatery is more like it.' He followed me into a large living-room whose walls were conspicuously bare of adornment, except for three flying ducks on one wall.

'That was Eric's little joke.' George saw me looking at them. 'Against Hamish, the snob. Poor Eric—' The sound he made was half-hiccough, half-sob. 'I talked to Eric, but now he's dead.'

'That's very sad.' To think that I had ever thought of George as a non-speaking extra; now it seemed that he couldn't stop, except—

'Had Eric stopped speaking to Hamish and Sebastian, too?'

' 'Course he had. Not nice people, Ham and Seb. Put up a good front at first, but when you got to know them . . . Have another drink.'

'Oh, I don't—'

''S'all right. It's Hamish's liquor.' He flourished a bottle of a very expensive brand at me. 'Nothing but the best for Hamish—no matter who pays.' He replenished his glass and, as an afterthought, poured a drink for me.

'Hamish notices any is gone—' He winked at me—'I'll say you drank it. I was entertaining you. He can't argue with that. He's got to keep on your good side.'

'Why?' This was news to me. 'I didn't realize Hamish cared about my opinion of him.'

'Oh, yes.' George slumped into a chair, nearly spilling his drink in the process. 'Your opinion's important to him. Very important.' He nodded sagely and winked at me again.

'But why? Is he hoping to become my financial adviser, too? Nigel has already put his bid in.' What mystified me was why anyone in the financial shape these people seemed to be in thought they were qualified to advise anyone else as to what to do with their money.

'Ah, good old Nigel. Never misses a trick—except the most important ones.' He slumped lower in his chair and seemed about to go to sleep. 'Poor old Nigel . . . poor old Sandra . . . poor old Eric . . .' He trailed off into silence. I waited for a while but he didn't stir. In fact, there was no sign of life.

'George . . . ? George . . . ?' There wasn't even a twitch. For a nervous moment I looked at my half-finished drink. Had I been ridiculously trusting to have swallowed any of it? Hamish seemed not to be the best-liked person around here. Had someone tampered with his liquor supply?

'George!' I raised my voice half an octave. 'George!'

He gave a muffled grunt and the glass slipped from his hand, the remaining liquid spilling across the carpet. He shifted position slightly and began a soft snoring.

That was that, and I hadn't even got round to

mentioning the party. With a sigh, I got up and retrieved his glass, mopping up the pool of Scotch with a couple of my own paper handkerchiefs. I wandered into the kitchen with the two glasses, rinsed them and left them in the sink, then looked around with interest.

The kitchen was actually recognizable as one; no State-of-the-Art, high-tech nonsense here. I also recognized the Official Seal on one of the back doors. So their kitchen also opened out on to the abyss, but from a lower level. If it hadn't been for that seal, I could have opened the door and checked the distance.

Evangeline wouldn't have hesitated, but I was made of more law-abiding stuff. With a sigh of regret, I turned and left The Chummery—or The Hatery. I still had an excuse for returning later and talking to the others, since I hadn't been able to issue my invitations.

Meanwhile, there were other invitations to deliver. And a couple of other flats I had been longing to get a closer look at.

'Ah!' Nigel seemed no more initially pleased to find me on his doorstep than George had been, but he had better manners. He was also sober.

'Ah, do come in. I'm afraid the place isn't up to scratch just now, but Sandra took care of organizing the cleaners.' He shook his head dazedly. ''I don't even know the name of the company or where they can be reached.'

'I won't stay long,' I promised, following him into a room as empty as our penthouse had originally been. Telltale marks on the carpet showed that it had once contained a lot more furniture. A swift assessment convinced me that more pieces were missing than could be accounted for by the contributions to our comfort.

'Ah! Quite all right.' Nigel looked around as though see-ing the place through my eyes and winced slightly. 'Ah, Sandra sent the suite away to be reupholstered. I'm expecting it back any time now. Afraid the place looks a little barren without it.'

'Uh-huh.' I had known enough jobless actors to have no difficulty in translating this into the truth: he had been selling off the furniture. The question was: had he done it while Sandra was still living with him or after her disappearance?

Probably the latter, since Sophie had accused him of living off Sandra. When she was no longer around to pay the bills, desperation must have set in.

'Can I offer you a drink? A cup of tea? Anything?' Nigel was anxious to distract me from my mental inventory. 'No trouble at all.'

'Nothing, thank you. I just dropped by to invite you to a party—' Belatedly, I realized anew that Nigel, as one of the bereaved, might not consider such an occasion appropriate at this time.

'That is,' I qualified hastily, 'it will be more of just a little gathering. A buffet meal and a few drinks. I feel it's the least I can do to repay all the kindness everyone has shown us ever since we moved in.'

'Ah! Not necessary. Not necessary at all.'

'Oh, but I want to. Really, I do.'

'Ah, well! If you feel that way . . .' Nigel was not offended, I saw, but rather pleased. His meals had probably been scrappy and unsatisfactory for a long while.

I filled him in on the details, accepted his thanks and headed for my next vict— I mean, prospective guest.

'A party? Me?' Mariah was not quite so incredulous this time around. She probably had me marked down as a fully-fledged eccentric, friendly but harmless. 'You're sure?'

'Quite sure.' Her flat was charming and well-furnished; no missing pieces of furniture or paintings here. Nothing from this flat had been volunteered to help feather our penthouse nest. Something tugged at the edge of my consciousness . . . the wisp of an idea beckoning me to follow it through to its logical conclusion.

'Then, thank you. I'd like to come.' She was still wary. 'If you're sure the others won't mind.'

'It's *my* party!' I was exasperated into tactlessness, but tried to recover my social graces. 'And I'm sure no one will mind. Why should they?'

'You really don't know, do you?' She gave a wry smile. 'They call me Mariah the Pariah. They—they hate me!'

'Oh, I'm sure you're exaggerating.'

'No, I'm not. You've seen the way they treat me. They can't bear to be in the same room with me!' Abruptly, she was on the verge of tears. 'And I only want to do what's best for them. I want to help, but they won't let me.'

That could explain a lot. People who wanted to be helpful were seldom appreciated as they thought they ought to be.

'If only they'd ask me,' she wailed. 'I can't stand to see them getting in deeper and deeper—' The tears began to flow and she became incoherent.

'Let me get you a glass of water.' I hastily escaped to the kitchen to give her time to regain her composure. She was usually so self-possessed, even when faced with all the slights and snubs from the others, that it was quite unnerving to see her break down like this.

'I'm all right,' I heard her choke out defensively, just before she settled down to some steady sobbing.

I realized, with an icy little chill down my spine, that the sound was familiar, very familiar.

Mariah had been the source of that wild unrestrained sobbing we had heard on the day of Eric's death. Had she been mourning him? Or had she been responsible for his death? Sent over the edge by one slight too many and then caught by remorse and terror as she realized what she had done?

Or had she simply been having herself an innocent crying

fit, overwhelmed by the accumulation of mute insults from people who had once been her friends? The way the others treated her was enough to set a saint howling.

'Here—' I hoped she didn't notice that my hand trembled as I held the glass of water out to her. 'Drink this and you'll feel better.'

'Thank you.' She swallowed it in great gulps, then dabbed at her eyes. 'I'm sorry, I'm so sorry. I don't know what you must think.'

'For heaven's sake, stop apologizing! I'm on your side. I think it's abominable the way the others treat you. How dare they?'

'Oh, they're not so bad, really,' she defended them, blowing her nose. 'They could be a lot more unpleasant, if they wanted. But they're afraid.'

'Afraid?'

'Of me. Of what I am. Of what I might do—' Her voice began to quaver again. 'I wouldn't. I never would. But I can't make them believe that.'

'Afraid of you?' She wasn't a person to inspire terror, sitting huddled there in her chair, damp handkerchief clutched in her hand. 'What could you do to anyone?'

'Not to anyone,' she said. 'Only to someone in the position most of them are in. You see, I work for . . . well, they specialize in bankruptcy and insolvency cases.'

'I see.' Quite a lot was becoming clear.

'I could give them so much helpful advice—' her tone was pleading—'but they won't ask me for help—or even talk to me. I think they're afraid I'm some sort of spy and I'll run back and report everything I find out—' She bit her lip and took a deep breath. 'I never would, but I don't know how to convince them of that. So everyone keeps avoiding me.'

Mariah the Pariah. We'd had our pariahs in Hollywood, too. Successful actors had been afraid to fraternize with those down on their luck, just in case the bad luck rubbed off on them. It was the same principle. Nothing changes.

'But you'll come to the party?' I persisted. 'Stick with Evangeline and me, if you want to. We'll take care of you. And Lazlo will be there.' I remembered that she had been his luncheon guest the other week. 'Lazlo is your friend, isn't he?'

'Yes,' she said consideringly. 'Yes, I believe he is. And I believe he may be right about some of the advice he's given me. He wants me to join his firm, you know. Perhaps the others would like me again if I changed my job.'

'It might help,' I admitted. I decided not to tell her that Lazlo had also offered Evangeline a job—there was no point in undermining her confidence in a prospective employer.

'It's better than the only other offer I've had recently.' She gave a short bitter laugh. 'They'd like to have me at the Serious Fraud Office.' The laugh threatened to turn into hysteria. 'That would really set the cat amongst the pigeons.'

'Pigeons?' I prompted hopefully, but I had gone too far. She stopped laughing abruptly.

'Thank you, I *will* come to your party. You're very kind.' Mariah rose to her feet, her tone had changed to one of dismissal. 'I'm sure you must have a great deal to do organizing your party. I mustn't monopolize you any longer.'

'Oh, uh—' Her sudden brusque change in attitude took me by surprise, making me wonder if Evangeline had been right and there was a touch of schizophrenia there some-where. If this was her customary attitude towards visitors, there might be more reason than her job for people treating her strangely. What seemed like snubs might just be caution.

'Yes, I do have quite a lot to do.' I let her escort me to

the door and heard it closed firmly behind me. Just the same, I decided to give her the benefit of the doubt—she'd obviously been through a lot—and resolved to have a quiet word with Jasper and make sure that he paid some attention to Mariah at the party. Whether he liked it or not, he had a certain responsibility to the residents of his building. I also decided to deliver the rest of the invitations by telephone.

It was as well that Evangeline wasn't around when I got back to the penthouse because she might have felt that I was infringing on her territory if she discovered that my first call was going to be to Superintendent Heyhoe.

Along with issuing the invitation, there was something I wanted to ask him.

CHAPTER 18

'Be nice to Mariah?' Jasper looked at me as though I had asked him to saunter into the lions' den and cozy up to the one with dripping jaws crouched over the bleeding carcass. 'Be *especially* nice to Mariah? You don't know what you're asking.'

'It shouldn't be so hard. She's young, pretty, intelligent—' Like a matchmaker, I began listing Mariah's assets. 'With a sweet personality—'

His mouth twisted and I wondered if I had gone too far.

I looked across to where Mariah stood smiling and drinking with Lazlo and Eddie, the taxi driver. They all seemed perfectly happy.

The party, if not in full swing, was ticking over nicely. Evangeline was in her element, swanning from group to group, dispensing graciousness and more drink. If I wasn't careful, people were going to mistake her for the hostess.

I moved over to intercept her as she headed for the next group. She greeted me with an approving nod.

'They're all getting relaxed and dropping their guards,' she said. 'Keep the liquor flowing and we could crack this case tonight.'

'This is supposed to be a party,' I said. 'Not the *Perry Mason Show*.'

'Don't quibble, Trixie, you know what I mean.'

'It isn't an episode from *The Happy Couple*, either.' My heart sank as I saw that I wasn't getting through to her. I just wanted everyone to have a good time; she was hell-bent on putting someone behind bars.

'That's better.' She was looking over my shoulder and I turned to see Superintendent Heyhoe getting out of the lift.

The noise level dipped drastically. Heads turned and people moved closer together, like wagon trains drawing into a circle against the enemy. I was glad that, on mature reflection, I had changed my mind about inviting Inspector Crichton: he probably wouldn't have been able to come, anyway. There were guidelines, if not rules, about socializing with the suspects.

'Superintendent Heyhoe—' I moved swiftly to greet him, cutting out Evangeline by a short head—'I'm so glad you could make it.'

'Thank you.' He wasn't so rapturous about it himself.

'My dear Hoo-Doo—' Evangeline decided to upstage me by bestowing a kiss on him; he barely flinched—'you must come and meet the others—' She slipped a hand under his arm and tried to draw him away.

'I met them the last time,' he said unenthusiastically, standing firm, so that Evangeline had either to relinquish his arm or be reduced to tugging at him. 'I want to have a word with Miss Dolan right now.'

'Well!' Evangeline tossed her head and stepped back. 'If I'm not *wanted*—'

He did not deny it. The silence lengthened pointedly.

'Well!' Evangeline turned on her heel and stalked off.

'With regard to your inquiry,' Heyhoe said to me as soon as she was out of earshot. 'There was no record of damage to vehicles reported in this area by any of the residents of this building.'

'But . . .' I met his eyes. 'Wouldn't an insurance company require a police report on the incident? If the owner wanted to claim on his insurance, that is?'

'They would.' Heyhoe regarded me sombrely, waiting for me to make some connection, or perhaps tell him a bit more about it.

'If the cars—and they were expensive cars—were badly damaged, enough to require garage repairs at some length, then the police should have been notified . . .' However strong anyone's desire not to get mixed up with the police, reporting incidents of this type was an absolute necessity if they intended to collect on their insurance—and no one in this building had given the impression that they could afford to absorb the cost of repairs themselves.

'That's right,' Heyhoe encouraged.

'So, if this vandalism wasn't reported, then . . .'

'It probably never happened,' he finished.

We regarded each other thoughtfully for a moment.

'But why should they lie about it?' It was a silly question; I knew as soon as I had asked it. Saving face was as important to a Yuppie as it had been to an Oriental Mandarin.

The question was: 'What really happened to their cars? Do you think they've sold them and don't want to admit it?'

'They don't want to admit it, all right.' Heyhoe seemed to realize that we were the centre of some attention; he threw back his head and laughed heartily, as though I had just told him an uproarious joke. The atmosphere in the room brightened immediately and the noise level began to rise again.

'Given the circumstances here—' Heyhoe spoke without moving his lips and still smiling—'my guess would be repossession.'

'Repo—?' But it made perfect sense. Almost everyone was in some financial trouble here. It was not unknown for those who failed to keep up the payments on their expensive toys to lose those toys. It even explained the excessive resentment against Jasper for not building the secure underground garage. Expensive vehicles left out on the street were too easily exposed to the danger of repossession as well as vandalism. But vandalism was the more socially acceptable explanation.

'Ladies and gentlemen—' Frederick had decided to act as impromptu toastmaster. 'Let us all raise our glasses to our charming hostess and, I hope I may say, good friend: Trixie Dolan!'

There were the usual 'Hear, hears' and I hoped I didn't look as guilty as I felt. Someone here wasn't going to consider me a good friend for much longer.

'You don't have a drink.' Mariah remedied that for Heyhoe with an untroubled smile. She was obviously the only person here who could look a Superintendent of Police in the eye without a qualm. Or perhaps she relished the thought that she was no longer the only pariah at the party.

'Mariah, dear.' I caught her arm before she could disappear again. 'Entertain our friend for a few minutes, will you? I have to have a word with someone.'

'Of course, that was always a strong possibility,' Evangeline said, as though she had suspected it all along. 'And it gives rise to even more possibilities.' She looked around at the happy guests, who were relaxing and getting into the swing of the party now that Heyhoe could be considered a paper tiger.

'New vistas, Trixie,' she murmured, her eyes narrowing as Sophie and Frederick began carrying in the platters of Tournedos Rossini. 'New vistas . . .'

All went well until it was time to transfer to *The Gliding Gourmet* for dessert, coffee and liqueurs. Frederick found it difficult to get the guests moving. They seemed curiously reluctant to leave the shelter of the building and venture across the narrow street to the boat.

'They're having too good a time.' Evangeline was disapproving. She looked as though she might be thinking of a way to stop that.

'For heaven's sake, leave them alone,' I said hastily. 'They've been having a hard time, they deserve a little fun.'

'*One* of them doesn't,' she said darkly.

'That's Inspector Crichton's problem.'

'Will you say that if someone else is murdered?'

'You don't think—?' Instinctively, I looked for George. I don't know why my subconscious had noted him as the victim type. But he was safely slumped against the far wall, a freshly filled glass in his hand, deep in conversation with Eddie—presumably one of the few people at the party he was willing to speak to.

'A person who has already killed twice has an awful lot to lose.' Evangeline followed my look, her gaze lingered for a moment on George, then flicked away dismissively.

'Come along, you lot!' Frederick tried again. 'The party's not ending, just changing location. Over to *The Gliding Gourmet* for the dessert buffet and coffee and liqueurs.'

'Ah! He's on a sticky wicket,' Nigel snickered, appearing beside us. 'No one wants to move away from here.'

'The party *is* going well,' I agreed.

'Nothing to do with the party,' Nigel said. 'Dangerous

outside. The werewolves are prowling.' He nodded sagely several times. 'Mustn't get caught by them. Mustn't let them in. Could lose everything. Could lose your life.'

'What do you mean?' But, still nodding sagely, he was already drifting on to the next group.

'He's drunk,' Evangeline said. '*In vino* there may be a bit of *veritas*, however. Don't let him get away.'

We caught him in a pincers movement just as he was closing in on Roz and Jasper. Each of us took an arm and swung him over beside the large arched window looking down on the entrance.

'Ah!' He seemed resigned rather than surprised at finding himself pinioned between us. He stared broodingly down on the street.

In the darkness, just beyond the radiance of the street-lamp, something moved and retreated.

'Is that your werewolf?' Evangeline asked.

'Werewolf? Werewolf?' Abruptly, he was almost sober. 'I don't know what—ah, we're talking about your new film, are we?' He arranged his features into a social smile. 'I can't wait to see it.'

'Never mind that,' Evangeline said. 'I want to know what—'

'Ah, what?' His features went slack and he swayed slightly. 'What, indeed?'

'I told Frederick he was being too free with the drinks!' Sophie had suddenly joined us. She stared at Nigel with contempt. 'The sooner everyone gets over to the boat and has some coffee, the better.'

'Don't want coffee,' Nigel muttered. 'Don't want to go out. Want to go to sleep.'

'Open the window.' I looked for the lock release. 'Some air might help.'

'No!' Nigel was galvanized into action; he spreadeagled

himself against the window defensively. 'Don't open it! Don't let them in!'

'Let who in? Who *is* that out there?' Evangeline leaned against the window pane peering out into the darkness. 'What are you afraid of?'

'He's afraid of everything,' Sophie sneered. 'And with good reason.'

'You belt up!' Nigel turned on her.

'Where's Frederick?' I turned and scanned the room for him. They were at each other's throats again. Frederick had promised he wasn't going to let this happen.

'My dear Trixie, a most excellent party.' Lazlo had caught my gesture of distress. He materialized at my side, along with Heyhoe and Mariah. 'You are to be congratulated—and thanked.'

'Very nice.' Heyhoe didn't sound so sure. He looked at Nigel suspiciously. 'Everything all right here?'

Sophie saw Frederick approaching and melted away to join him.

'Just fine.' I smiled brightly and wriggled my eyebrows at Heyhoe, trying to signal that he was sounding a little too professional. 'We're attempting to get the party across to the boat now. Perhaps, if we provide a lead . . .'

'Good idea.' Evangeline took an iron grip on Nigel's arm and started for the main staircase to the lobby. 'Come along, everybody,' she called. 'On to the next course.'

With varying degrees of enthusiasm, the others rallied and followed her lead. Nigel was the only one actively struggling to hold back, but he underestimated Evangeline's strength and determination. At the head of staircase, she turned and said something inaudible. Superintendent Heyhoe instantly leaped forward to stand close on Nigel's other side, looking menacing. Nigel stopped struggling.

I let everyone go ahead of me and brought up the rear with Lazlo and Mariah. Downstairs, Hamish and Sebastian seemed to be standing as a sort of Guard of Honour on either side of the open front door as the others streamed through it and across the street. I could see Frederick and Sophie standing in the doorway of the dining salon to greet them. All seemed to be going well again.

We had just started through the doorway when Sebastian gave a shout and pushed past us. Hamish pounded after him.

'There he goes!' Sebastian bellowed. 'Yoiks! Tally ho!'

'Oh, God!' Mariah moaned. 'We've got to stop them! They'll do something desperate.' She took off after them.

The rallying call had halted the others in their progress towards *The Gliding Gourmet*. They turned and joined in the chase.

'What is going on?' Lazlo asked as the field streamed past us. 'Is it some English party game?'

'It's blood sports, mate,' Eddie panted, grabbing our arms and pulling us with him. 'They're going to kill the poor bastards!'

'Not while I'm around!' Heyhoe snapped. He and Evangeline shot past us with a turn of speed I hadn't thought her capable of; adrenaline is a wonderful thing.

We followed the sound of baying throats down the street, around several corners and into a cul-de-sac where they had trapped their prey. Two men were huddled against a wall, trying to face down their maddened pursuers.

'They've got him!' I recognized the taller man. 'It's the Prowler!'

'Prowler, my eye,' Eddie said. 'Don't you know a bailiff when you see one?'

'String 'em up!' someone shouted.

'Throw 'em in the river!' was a counter-proposal.

'We'll teach them to hang around here.' Hamish advanced menacingly.

'We're only doing our job,' one of them whined.

'Are you?' Mariah stepped forward. 'Then you'll be able to produce identification—'

They nodded eagerly, hands going towards their pockets.

'And a copy of Regulation 39,' Mariah went on. 'Plus Schedule 55 of the Enforcement Regulations 1989—'

Most of their eagerness disappeared. They looked at each other and then at Mariah.

'As well as a copy of the charges connected with the distress,' she concluded. 'Each and every distress,' she added firmly.

They were beaten and they knew it. They looked at her and at the furious mob behind her.

'Don't let them get away!' Unconsciously, Hamish echoed Evangeline. 'We've got the buggers dead to rights! Let's teach them a lesson!'

'The river!' Sebastian started up the cry again.

'Don't let them do it.' The prowling bailiff appealed to Mariah.

'No one's going to do anything.' Superintendent Heyhoe moved forward to stand beside Mariah. He gave Hamish the kind of look he usually gave Evangeline, then turned it on the cowering bailiffs. 'Clear out!'

'And don't come back!' Hamish thundered at their departing backs.

'That's right!' Evangeline was not to be left out. 'And never darken our doors again!'

Against my better judgement, I chose something deeply chocolatey from the dessert buffet and stood deliberating as to whether I should pour some of the ubiquitous heavy cream over it.

'That was very good of you,' I heard Jasper saying to Mariah in the queue behind me.

Really! I thought in irritation. He could at least have

said, 'You're beautiful when you're angry.' Hadn't he ever
seen any of his grandfather's old films?

'I *am* on your side, you know,' Mariah said softly. 'I wish
you'd believe that. I *would* like to help.'

'Yes. Yes, I . . . I *do* believe it. I . . . I think perhaps we
should have a long talk tomorrow.'

'What's wrong with right now?' I glanced over my shoulder in time to see Mariah take him firmly by the arm and
lead him ashore.

Well, it was a nice mild evening; the moon was nearly
full and a stroll along the bank might do a lot towards
clearing up any misunderstandings. Given enough time,
Jasper might even remember the proper dialogue.

The party had resumed with renewed gaiety aboard *The
Gliding Gourmet*, everyone lifted to new heights of hilarity
by their triumph over the bailiffs. Which reminded me . . .

'What's all this about bailiffs?' I asked, as I joined Evangeline, Heyhoe and Eddie at their table. 'Who are they?
Why have they been hanging around here? And why was
everybody so afraid of them?'

'Basically, they're private debt collectors,' Heyhoe
began.

'They're a holdover from Victorian times,' Evangeline
said grimly. 'Absolutely Dickensian. They're allowed to go
into private homes—'

'Only if they're invited in,' Heyhoe interrupted. 'You
have no obligation to let them in and they can only effect
peaceable entry.'

'Which is why they were hanging around trying to sneak
in. And ringing our bell, hoping we'd let them in,' Evangeline said.

'And why everybody warned us to keep them out.' A lot
of things were becoming clear to me.

'Er, yes.' Heyhoe looked uncomfortable. 'Once inside,

bailiffs are allowed more powers. They can break down internal doors, even locked ones, in order to seize property to the value of the amount owed. Unfortunately, they sometimes remove too much. Of course, they can't always be sure how much the property will fetch at auction.'

'Break down doors?' I echoed incredulously. 'Seize property? What kind of property?'

'Anything of value that can be sold. Furniture, paintings, television sets, videos, jewellery—nothing is exempt except fittings and built-in furniture.' Heyhoe shifted uneasily under my gaze. 'It's the law.'

'As has been remarked before,' Evangeline said, 'the law is an ass.'

'But—' I still found it hard to believe—'for someone to be able to walk into your own home and help themselves to your belongings.'

'There will have been a Court Order issued first,' Heyhoe said defensively.

'Then people must know that the bailiffs will be coming to take away their possessions.' No wonder no one had wanted us to allow strangers into the building.

'Unless they've managed to acquire the money to pay off the debt first.' Heyhoe looked around at the increasingly festive activity. 'From the way they're celebrating, your friends obviously haven't. Those bailiffs won't be back again in a hurry, but others will eventually appear. This has only bought your friends more time.'

'Time to hide still more of their assets.' Evangeline looked at me and we both had the same thought. 'I suddenly see just why our friends have been so generous in furnishing our penthouse.'

'What the bailiffs can't find, they can't remove. And all this time—' I gave an elaborate sigh—'I thought it was for the sake of my big baby-blue eyes.'

'Not to mention our unique contribution to the world of

the cinema.' Evangeline gave a grimace. 'And our inesti-
mable value as an attraction to prospective buyers.'

'Oh, well.' My sigh was not so elaborate this time. 'One
more illusion shattered.'

'And one more mystery solved,' Evangeline said.

Heyhoe twitched, as though the suggestion of unsolved
mysteries was some sort of reflection on him. 'This is not
my—' he began.

'Why so solemn here?' Hamish appeared beside our table
waving a bottle and I looked at him with narrowed eyes.
I distinctly remembered deciding against champagne for
the party.

'My treat,' he said easily, interpreting my look. (But, if I
hadn't noticed, would it have been?) 'The enemy is routed.
Again. We need a *real* treat after all we've been through
lately.'

'Thank you,' I said coldly. So much for my party.

'Oh, I didn't mean that—'

'That's old Hamish, all right.' George came up behind
us, even more drunk than the last time I had seen him.
'Never means anything he says. Especially when he
promises to repay money.'

'You're drunk, as usual, George.' Hamish turned and
glared at him. 'Go away.'

'What if I don't?' George leered at him. 'What will you
do? Break up The Chummery? Buy us out and take it over
yourself? Chance would be a fine thing wouldn't it? And
solvency.'

'Pay no attention to him,' Hamish told us. 'He's drunk
now and unstable at the best of times.'

'As the pot said about the kettle,' Evangeline muttered.

'Sebastian's another.' George looked around vaguely.
'Where'sh'bastian? Got to keep your eye on him. Ev'ry
minute.'

I had last been aware of Sebastian when he was agitating

for the mob to throw the bailiffs into the river. He was nowhere in sight now. Mariah and Jasper were strolling along the riverside; did Sebastian still want to throw someone in? What was George trying to tell us?

'Which one is Sebastian?' Heyhoe asked with sudden interest.

'He's over in the corner talking to Roz,' Hamish said. 'Minding his own business, which is more than we could ever persuade George to do.'

'Couldn't 'suade Eric, either.' George gave a sly smile.

'I'm sorry about this,' Hamish apologized. 'I don't want to break up the party, but I think it would be best if we got George back to The Chummery to sleep it off.'

'The Hatery, you mean.' George shook his head. 'Everybody hates everybody else in The Chummery. Why not be honest? If you know how?'

'You see?' Hamish shrugged ruefully. 'First insults and the next stage is violence. I'm afraid George doesn't hold his liquor like a gentleman.'

'Violence?' Both Heyhoe and Evangeline quivered.

'Unhappily, yes.' Hamish signalled to Sebastian, who said something to Roz; they both came over to us.

Some of the others noticed them and began drifting in our direction as she began thanking me for a lovely party. A queue began to form behind her. With an inward sigh, I recognized the signs. Whether he had intended to or not, Hamish was breaking up the party. Even Eddie was deserting me.

The boat swayed gently as the departing guests stepped ashore. Frederick and Sophie turned the lights out in the gallery and dimmed the lights in the dining salon.

I found myself humming, '*The party's over . . .*'

CHAPTER 19

But the party wasn't quite over. Despite his stated intention, Hamish hadn't left. George had slumped to the floor and was lying inert, a dead weight as Hamish and Sebastian struggled to lift him upright.

'Shall we have a farewell drink?' Frederick approached, carrying a dusty bottle. 'On us. The last of a truly memorable cognac. To celebrate the end of a very successful party.'

'It *did* go well, didn't it?' Sophie set down a tray of balloon glasses and slid into a chair, awaiting the congratulations that were her due.

'Thanks to you. The catering was superb.' I cheerfully obliged.

Frederick poured the cognac, ignoring the unseemly tussle on the floor so expertly that I realized it must be a familiar end to many an evening. I wondered if Eric . . . ?

'Smashing party . . . smashing food.' Nigel hadn't left yet, either. He offered Sophie a tentative smile, but wasn't foolish enough to offer his hand. 'Bygones be bygones?'

'Since it's my sister who's gone—' Sophie stiffened. 'And you're—'

'Have a drink, old chap.' Frederick tried to be peacemaker.

'Sit down, Nigel.' I refrained from adding, *before you fall down*. One of them stretched out on the deck was enough.

Sophie sniffed and looked away as Nigel pulled up a chair. Evangeline and Heyhoe were still fascinated by the scene behind them. George had begun groaning, while Hamish and Sebastian kept trying to heave him on to his feet. Eventually the rough treatment seemed to rouse him, he muttered an incoherent protest.

'Perhaps they should throw *him* in the river,' Evangeline suggested tartly.

'Not a bad idea.' Nigel looked at the mêlée with disapproval. 'Might do all of them a bit of good. Never could see why Sandra put up with them. Louts in pinstripes, that's all they are.'

They had George on his feet now, half-draped over Sebastian.

'Can you manage?' Hamish asked. 'Off you go, then. I'll be along in a minute.'

Sebastian nodded and lurched out of the door with George.

'Terribly sorry about that.' Hamish came over to us. 'I'm afraid old George is getting more out of control every day. We'll have to do something about it soon before—' He pointedly avoided looking at Heyhoe. 'Before anyone else does.'

Was he implying that George was the murderer? Or was he setting up George as the fall guy? I wasn't the only one to look askance at Hamish. From the expression on Heyhoe's face, he had forgotten all consideration of jurisdiction.

'Just what do you mean by that?' Evangeline was on the scent.

'I didn't realize they were so friendly with Sandra.' At the same time, Sophie spoke. She had obviously been reflecting on Nigel's remarks.

'Sandra was generous with her money.' Nigel had been thinking it over, too. 'Too generous. Everybody was trying to borrow from her. Not likely old Hamish would be an exception. Always an eye for the main chance, old Hamish. How much did she loan you?' He looked at Hamish sharply.

'Not a penny, old man,' Hamish said smoothly, too smoothly.

'Are you sure?' Evangeline didn't trust him, either.

'Did anyone find an IOU from me among her belongings? Did anyone find any record naming me at all?' Hamish spread his hands. 'There you are.'

From outside, there came a howl and a splash. 'Man overboard!' someone shouted.

'Oh, God—there goes George!' Frederick led the pack as we raced from ship to shore. Two figures teetered on the edge of the retaining wall, locked in combat.

'Break it up!' Frederick and Heyhoe moved to separate them. I stood well clear, relieved that the shout of 'Man overboard!' had been premature. And yet, there had been that splash . . .

'Don't just stand there, Trixie!' Evangeline panted. 'Help me!' She was battling to restrain Sophie from joining in the fray.

'Take it easy.' I caught Sophie's other arm and pulled her back. 'Let's be female chauvinist sows and let the men handle this. It won't do you any good to get a black eye.'

'Quite right,' Evangeline agreed. 'Let Hoo-Ha arrest everybody and sort it out back at the police station. That's the way we always did it in *The Happy*—'

Sophie gave a loud piercing scream. I had every sympathy. I often felt that way myself when Evangeline began on her reminiscences of *The Happy Couple*.

'Stop them!' Sophie shrieked. 'Stop them!'

But they already had the combatants safely subdued. Frederick clutching Sebastian and Heyhoe grappling with George, they were moving back to join us. Then I followed the direction of Sophie's pointing finger.

The Gliding Gourmet was gliding out into midstream.

'My God!' Frederick let go of Sebastian and dashed to the pierhead, staring helplessly as the boat was swept into the current of the outgoing tide. 'They've set her adrift!'

'George did it,' Sebastian said defensively. 'I tried to stop him.'

So that was the splash I heard: the mooring rope being thrown into the river.

'Ahoy the *Gourmet*!' Heyhoe let George fall and stepped up beside Frederick, cupping his hands to his mouth and shouting across the water. 'Ahoy the *Gourmet*! You're adrift! Start your engine and steer for the shore.'

'They can't!' Sophie burst into tears. 'We haven't *got* an engine. We took it out to make more room for the kitchen.'

'Serve Hamish right,' George mumbled. 'Killed Sandra, killed Eric. Filthy temper . . . always hitting . . . pushing people.'

'Killed Sandra?' Sophie stopped crying. 'Hamish killed Sandra!'

'Had fight.' George nodded solemnly. 'Wanted some of her money back. Not all, just some. Hamish didn't want to . . . had it invested, he said. Got quite argumentative, the way he does, then hit her with his briefcase—brassbound edges, you know. Hit too hard. Then it was too late. Put her in river . . .'

'You knew all this?' Heyhoe was outraged. 'And you didn't tell the police?'

'Eric knew. Found out. Eric picked up wrong briefcase other day, found traces of blood. Thought it was rust at first, but brass doesn't rust. Told me about it. Was going to tell police, but must have talked to Hamish first. Goodbye, Eric. 'f'I told—Goodbye, George.'

'You see,' Frederick said triumphantly to Sophie. 'I told you Nigel was innocent. He'd never have harmed Sandra.'

'Nigel!' Sophie shrieked. 'Oh, Frederick, he's still on board!'

'What?'

'He pulled Hamish back when the rest of us rushed ashore. I heard him say he wanted to talk to him.'

'He must have been putting two and two together,' Evangeline surmised. 'Now he's trapped in a drifting boat with a killer.' She spoke with some relish, it was a situation worthy of *The Happy Couple*.

The *Gourmet* was gliding ever faster downstream, rocking from side to side, as though there might be a fight going on below deck.

'Thames Barrier, here he comes!' George mumbled happily before passing out again.

'*Do* something!' Unreasonably, Evangeline turned on Heyhoe. 'You're the law! It's up to you to do something!'

'We'd better get inside to a telephone,' Heyhoe said, 'and I'll notify the river police. Since,' he added nastily, 'your friend's cellphone is rather out-of-reach at the moment.'

'Oh, don't worry about that.' Evangeline opened her handbag. 'I have my own now.' She handed it to him.

A bellow of rage exploded across the water as Heyhoe spoke tersely into the phone.

A figure stood on the deck of *The Gliding Gourmet* and stared about wildly before moving over to the rail.

'No!' Frederick shouted. 'No! The current is too strong. Stay where you are! The river police are on their way. They'll get you . . .' His voice died away as the figure jumped.

'That was Hamish, I'm sure,' Sophie said. 'But where's Nigel?'

'Better off, if he's still aboard,' Frederick said.

We watched in helpless silence as Hamish battled the current. He was too far away for us to throw him a life preserver, although Sebastian was wrenching frantically at one fixed to the pierhead. Hamish was travelling down river a lot faster than *The Gliding Gourmet*.

'Old Hamish never was much of a swimmer,' Sebastian said sadly, 'not even at school.'

*

'What is it? What's happened?' Jasper and Mariah came running along the river walk as the police boat towed *The Gliding Gourmet* back to its mooring. I was pleased to see that Mariah's lipstick was well-smudged.

Some of the others had returned to the scene, drawn by the noise and activity. Another police boat was proceeding slowly down river, searchlights sweeping the surface of the water, looking for what we could only fear was a body.

Evangeline filled them in on events with gusto, while I waited anxiously with Sophie and Frederick as the police helped Nigel ashore.

'I'm all right,' Nigel said unsteadily. 'He knocked me out—perhaps he thought he'd killed me. When I came to, a policeman was bending over me. Afraid I'm not as good a boxer as I thought. Silly of me to stick to Marquess of Queensbury Rules. No one else does.'

'That's one fight you were lucky to lose,' Frederick said. 'Otherwise, you might have been tempted to swim for the shore, like Hamish.'

'Where *is* Hamish?' Nigel looked around dazedly.

'Never mind him right now, old chap.' Frederick steadied Nigel. 'Let's get you to bed. Everything else can wait until morning.'

'Come with us. Nigel,' Sophie said. 'We'll take care of you.' They led him away, puzzled but unprotesting.

'Right!' Inspector Crichton, who had been conducting a teeth-baring travesty of politeness with Superintendent Heyhoe while Heyhoe tried to explain just how it was that he had wound up solving Crichton's case, turned on Sebastian and George with pent-up ferocity. 'You two can come along to the station and start helping us with our inquiries. There are quite a few explanations we'd like from you.'

Slowly, the spectators sorted themselves out and made their way back into the building. The searchlights of the police boat were mere slivers of light as they disappeared around a bend of the river.

'Well,' Evangeline sighed. 'I guess the excitement's over. We might as well turn in for the night.'

'What's left of it,' I agreed. There was already the brightness of dawn on the horizon. There was also a strange ringing in my ears.

'Who could be calling at this hour?' Evangeline fished out her cellphone and stared at it incredulously. 'Hello?'

Her face changed. 'It's for *you*,' she said indignantly, handing it over.

'Mother?' It was Martha's voice, warm and vibrant and happy. 'Mother, we're on our way home.'

'This morning?' I asked with a faint qualm. There went my plans to sleep late and have a lazy day.

'Not quite. In two or three days. We're stopping in Paris first.'

'Wonderful!' I looked up to see Evangeline pause in the entrance. Now I knew what it reminded me of: one of the great cinematic palaces of the 'thirties.

Evangeline gave a wave then turned and spread herself across the doorway in a libellous parody of Griselda. I began to giggle.

'Mother, are you all right?'

'Just fine, darling,' I said. 'Absolutely marvellous. How's Hugh? And the children?'

She began to tell me. I strolled across the street, listening to her voice with a feeling of great contentment.

The long night was over, Evangeline wasn't really too annoyed with me, and Martha was on her way home with her family.

Life was getting back to what passed for normal.